THE TRAIL

MEIKA HASHIMOTO

SCHOLASTIC

Garfield Ridge
Shelter

Kinsman Pond
Shelter

Lonesome
Lake Hut

THE KINSMANS

FRANCONIA RIDGE

WHITE

VERMONT
NEW HAMPSHIRE

Velvet Rocks
Shelter

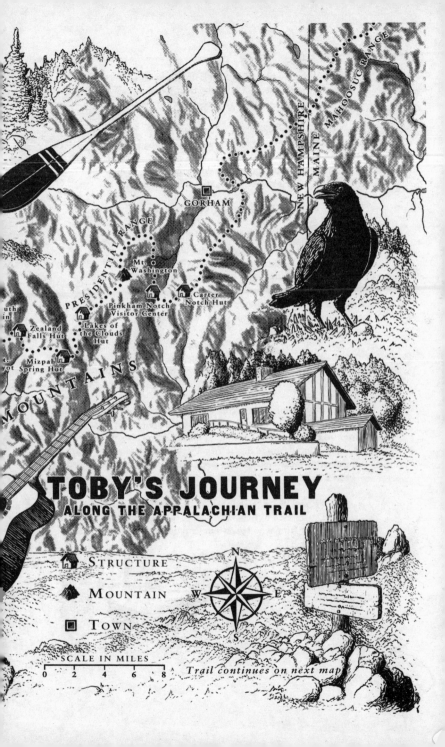

MAHOOSUC RANGE

NEW HAMPSHIRE | MAINE

GORHAM

PRESIDENTIAL RANGE

Mt.
Washington

Pinkham Notch
Visitor Center

Carter
Notch Hut

uth
in

Zealand
Falls Hut

Lakes of
the Clouds
Hut

Mizpah
yot Spring Hut

MOUNTAINS

TOBY'S JOURNEY
ALONG THE APPALACHIAN TRAIL

STRUCTURE

MOUNTAIN

TOWN

N

W   E

S

SCALE IN MILES

0   2   4   6   8

Trail continues on next map

Published in the UK by Scholastic Children's Books, 2020
Euston House, 24 Eversholt Street, London, NW1 1DB
A division of Scholastic Limited

London – New York – Toronto – Sydney – Auckland
Mexico City – New Delhi – Hong Kong

SCHOLASTIC and associated logos are trademarks and/or
registered trademarks of Scholastic Inc.

First published in the US by Scholastic Inc., 2017

Text © Meika Hashimoto, 2017
Book design by Mary Claire Cruz
Map art © John Stevenson, 2017
Bear silhouette ©: Shutterstock, Inc./eva_mask

The right of Meika Hashimoto to be identified as the author of this work has
been asserted by her under the Copyright, Designs and Patents Act 1988.

ISBN 978 0702 30203 9

A CIP catalogue record for this book is available from the British Library.

Printed by CPI Group (UK) Ltd, Croydon, CR0 4YY
Papers used by Scholastic Children's Books are made
from wood grown in sustainable forests.

1 3 5 7 9 10 8 6 4 2

www.scholastic.co.uk

To my father, Toshio Hashimoto,
who taught me to love the mountains

TOBY'S JOURNEY
ALONG THE APPALACHIAN TRAIL

🏠 STRUCTURE

⛰ MOUNTAIN

◻ TOWN

N
W · E
S

SCALE IN MILES
0 2 4 6 8 10

Bates
Ridge

EUSTIS RIDGE

FLAGSTAFF
LAKE

Mt.
Bigelow

WYMAN
LAKE

Sugarloaf
Mtn.

RANGELEY

Poplar
Ridge

Brimstone
Mtn.

MAHOOSUC RANGE

NEW HAMPSHIRE
MAINE

Trail continues from previous map

CHAPTER 1

OUT IN THE woods, all by myself, I've become aware of the little things. There are the good littles: cooling my face with a handful of water from a mountain stream. The way sunlight plays through wind-rippled leaves. The startled leap of a deer that only I see.

Then there are the bad littles: mosquitoes, mostly. Achy feet. Lying down on a sharp rock under the tent after a long day of hiking, being too tired to move, and waking up to a bruise the size of a baseball on my shoulder.

But really. These are little things.

Then there are the little things that can turn into big things. I call them my keeps list. When I'm out on the trail, every hour or two I tick them off: (1) Keep warm. (2) Keep hydrated. (3) Keep eating. (4) Keep an eye on the sun.

Ignoring a little keep could turn into a big problem later. So I'll pull on a jacket if I'm cold, or slug back some water if I'm thirsty, or scarf down a Snickers if my belly rumbles. And I always try to make camp before dark.

It's a simple system, but I've learned the hard way that if you neglect one of the keeps long enough, before you know it, your teeth are chattering as you tilt back an aspirin for your dehydration headache, trying to make dinner in the pitch-dark with a groan in your stomach loud enough to wake the zombies.

In the woods, after dark, it's easy to believe in zombies.

But I know better than to be afraid of that.

Sort of.

Right now, I've been doing pretty good with my keeps list. It's evening, and I've pitched the tent by a small stream. Even though it's late June, I've layered up with a wool hat and two jackets—a light fleece and a waterproof shell. I've taken a long drink of water and have unpacked my mess kit to make dinner. Bowl, cup, fork. A quart pot with a lid that doubles as a frying pan.

Next, I break out my stove. It's an MSR PocketRocket, a pretty cool piece of camping equipment that folds to the size of my fist. I screw it onto my fuel canister and open the three pot supports. A quick twist of my wrist turns on the gas; I flick a match and, a second later, a bright blue flame darts up. I pour the rest of my water bottle into the pot and settle it onto the stove.

By the time the water has boiled, I've dug through my pack and found my meal for the night—a package of spaghetti and some ready-to-eat tomato sauce in a plastic pouch. It doesn't compare to what I'd be eating back at Gran's house, but I'm so hungry I don't care. I dump the spaghetti into the bubbling water. As the long, thick strands twist in the water, a burst of saliva floods my mouth.

I've been on the trail for just a few days but have enough food for only one more, two if I count my candy bars as full-on meals. I've been eating more than I expected. I'm going to need to find a gas station or grocery store on a real road soon to restock.

That's what I call them now: real roads. Gravel and tar with straight yellow lines that run true and smooth to their destinations. Sometimes when the bad littles are getting to me—I'm lying in the tent and a stray mosquito won't stop buzzing, or my pack strap presses right on my black-and-blue shoulder—I think about taking a real road. A real road would bring me home so fast. All I would need to do is follow one to a town and turn myself in to the police station. A few hours later, I would be home.

But taking a real road would mean giving up. And I can't do that. Not yet, not while there's something warped and unfinished inside me that can be drained away only by hiking, step-by-step, down this two-foot-wide path, into the wilderness for four hundred more miles, until I'm standing at the top of Mount Katahdin at the end of the Appalachian Trail.

Just when I am crouching over the boiling pot, calculating the last nuggets of food in my pack, I hear it. A growl in the shadows.

My heart slams into my throat.

Bear.

I've been so busy thinking about the little things that I lost sight of the big ones. A bear is a big thing. And not a good one.

I am alone, with only a Swiss Army knife for protection. And I'm pretty sure a two-inch blade covered in last night's cheese crumbs won't stop much of anything. But I slide the knife out of my back pocket anyway and point it out ahead of me, jabbing at the night.

The growl gets louder. It's coming from a choked tangle of bushes fifty feet from my campsite. In the thickening darkness I can't see when it might attack.

I think I read somewhere that if you see a black bear, you shouldn't run away or they'll think you're prey. You're supposed to look big and make loud noises. So I stand up slowly. I open my mouth to shout at it.

Nothing comes out.

I also read somewhere that animals can see and smell fear, which is really too bad because I'm trembling all over and I can feel myself breaking into a cold sweat. *Look big*, I tell myself again. *Be brave.* But then my mind empties and I'm just praying, *Please don't eat me, please don't eat me.*

Bristling fur. Sharp teeth. Snarling lips. I cry out as it comes hurtling from the bushes like a burst of crackling gunfire and—it's a dog. Shaggy-faced and flop-eared, eyes brave with desperation. Pitch-black except for a hollowed-out chest that's so mud-spattered, I can't tell if it's brown or white. A tail bent at the tip, as though someone had tried to snap it in half. He's definitely a mutt. Mangy and starving and as ugly as sin. I can count his ribs.

The dog rushes at me, but I feel my heart start beating again. I leap back as he stalks over to my cook site. A swift kick with his hind leg upsets my dinner pot.

"Hey!" I shout, but it's too late. Spaghetti and foaming starchy water spill to the ground. The movement was practiced, smooth. This dog has done this before. He must have seen me—a skinny kid with unwashed dark hair and terrified brown eyes who weighed less than a hundred pounds even with pockets full of change—and figured I was an easy target. He grabs a mouthful of scorching noodles and beats it back to the bushes.

I have never seen a dog hold boiling food in its mouth. The rest of my fear melts away. He must be near-crazy with hunger. I wonder how long he has been out here, scavenging for scraps from frightened hikers.

I stare at the remaining spaghetti lying in the dirt. My dinner. My stomach growls angrily. I can try to salvage the remains, give the noodles a long rinse and hope the tomato sauce covers up any leftover grit.

I sigh. Instead, I dig a fork out of my mess kit and scoop the muddy spaghetti into my pot. I tiptoe over to the edge of the campsite and dump the contents on the ground. I can see the dog now. He's twenty feet away, behind the thickest part of the bushes. He watches me with uncertain eyes.

I back up slowly. The dog does not budge until I have retreated all the way to the tent. Then he shuffles forward and begins gulping down the rest of his dinner.

"Enjoy it," I tell him. I'm still annoyed, but at least he seems to appreciate my cooking.

Digging into my pack, I pull out a flattened peanut-butter-and-jelly sandwich. It was going to be my lunch for tomorrow, but it will have to do for tonight. As the dog busies himself with my pasta, I put away the rest of my food and then crawl into the tent, where I spend the last minutes before true dark with the taste of cold sandwich in my mouth and the certainty that, tomorrow, I'm going to have to find more food.

CHAPTER 2

INSIDE THE TENT, the dark heavy all around me, I can't stop my thoughts from crowding back into my brain. It's easy to keep them out when I'm worrying about food or water, or putting one foot in front of the other. But here at night, I can't help thinking about the reason I'm here: my best friend. Lucas. It was Lucas's idea to hike the Appalachian Trail in the first place.

He had been my best friend ever since second grade, when I moved from my parents' house in the suburbs of Boston to my grandma's place up in Norwich, Vermont, to wait out their divorce. My parents and I had been driving up I-91 one rainy night when a moose jumped the guardrail. My dad rammed on the brakes, and the car had gone spinning.

From the backseat I had seen a whirl of dark fur and the tiny needles of the spruce trees that lined the highway. Fur, needles, fur, needles—we were out of control, and like a sped-up movie I watched the galloping animal come straight at me, its heavy body smashing like the Hulk's fist through the back door.

There was the crack of a shattering window, and I remember thinking how I never realized that car glass broke in twinkling cubes instead of jagged triangles.

The next couple of hours were fuzzy—there were blue-blazing sirens and the static of police radios clicking on and off, but nothing really came into focus until I was in the hospital with tubes up my nose and my arm in a cast and Gran by my side, telling me that I was going to be okay.

My parents were unhurt in the crash. They stayed in Vermont only long enough to make sure I would be okay and left before my week in the hospital was even over. I guess nearly losing their only son wasn't enough to distract them from the grief of losing their marriage.

On the third evening, a boy my age walked in, joking with the nurses as he climbed into the bed next to mine. He had a cast on his arm, like me, but it extended all the way down to his hand and fingers as well. He didn't seem to mind. He saw me looking at his arm and lightly patted the hard plaster of his cast. "Fell out of a tree. Never trust a dead branch." He nodded at me. "How did you get yours?"

"Car accident."

The boy went still. Then he swung his legs past the side of the bed and trotted over to me. He was barefoot.

I shuddered when I saw his toes curl against the tiles—what kind of kid would cross a hospital floor without shoes? His feet must have been freezing. The boy's deep blue eyes were filled with amazement. "You're the kid."

"The kid?" I asked.

"The moose kid. Norwich is a small town. Your grandma and my parents are friends. I heard about you and your folks at dinner last night." He gripped the side rail of my hospital bed with his good hand.

I looked at this boy, with his broken arm and chipper freckles, and all I could manage was a strangled "Yeah," before burying my head in my pillow. I had just been in an accident. Everything hurt. My parents had abandoned me. I didn't want to talk.

After a while I heard him remove his hand from the rail and return to his bed. He didn't speak to me again; the next morning he was gone. I figured I'd missed my chance to make a friend but couldn't really bring myself to care.

The day before I left the hospital, Gran handed me a plain white envelope. "This is from the next-door neighbor's son, Lucas," she told me.

The envelope contained a note in messy handwriting on plain white loose-leaf. It read: Hey Toby! I heard you're getting out of the hospital. I'll come by on Saturday at noon.

That Saturday I met him on Gran's front porch. He had a stack of DC comics with him. We didn't talk much, but we sat on the porch swing as cold spring rain soaked into the grass, and buried ourselves in the adventures of Batman and Superman and the Flash.

When I boarded the bus a week later for the first day of school, I was dreading the long walk past unfamiliar faces as I tried to find a seat. Then I saw someone standing in the back, waving wildly with his one good arm. Lucas, of course. We ended up riding the bus to Norwich Elementary School together every day, and by the end of the fall we were testing out our newly healed arms on bike rides and games of catch.

For three years, Lucas and I were inseparable. As I settled into Norwich and got to know other kids, sometimes I joined in on kickball games and freeze tag at recess. But most of the time it was just me and Lucas.

That first year, we spent endless afternoons exploring our backyards, but by fifth grade we were having adventures by local rivers and trees and mountains. We built forts with rocks and broken branches. We battled with sticks for swords. We watched the tadpoles shed their fishy tails to become full-throated bullfrogs.

Sometimes we'd swing bats in Norwich's perfectly measured ball fields, or go to a pool party in town, but our favorite thing to do was to go camping behind my house. Lucas's dad was a middle school teacher and a Boy Scouts leader, and he taught us all about survival in the woods, taking us for overnights during the summer when he was on vacation.

As I lie here thinking about it, I can almost pretend that that's where I am right now: a tent in the woods behind Gran's house. Lucas beside me. His dad in another tent just next to ours. I can almost feel their presence, and it helps me finally fall asleep.

CHAPTER 3

I WAKE TO light rain pattering down on the tent. It's snug and cozy in my mummy sleeping bag, and even though I know I should get up soon, I pull the hood over my head and burrow deeper inside.

Gran likes to say that the best temperature is bed. At this moment, I couldn't agree more. There is something miraculous about the fact that my own body turned yesterday's soggy peanut-butter-and-jelly sandwich into enough energy and heat to keep me sleeping comfortably through the night.

Curled in the darkness, I inhale my warmth for a few minutes more, not minding the smells that happen to a hiker—sweat, dirt, and last night's trapped farts. They're not pretty smells. But they're my smells.

Eventually, though, I know it's time to get up when my belly reminds me of the third thing on my keeps list: *Keep eating, Toby!* I wriggle out of my bag and rub away my eye crusts. My boots are under the vestibule, a patch of tent awning that keeps my belongings dry and covered. I unzip the door and poke my head out, scanning the campsite to see if that mangy dog is still hanging around.

He's not there. I reach out and pull my boots inside. My socks are draped over them, dirt-stiffened but not too damp. As I slide on a sock, a scraping jolt of pain hits my foot. I yelp. Blisters have formed on two of my toe knuckles, red-shiny and taut with fluid.

I dig through the top pocket of my pack and find my Swiss Army knife and Band-Aids from my first aid kit. I unfold one of the smaller blades from the knife. As I lean over to nick open my blisters, I hear a voice.

Toe, you're gonna have to sterilize that.

It's Lucas's voice. Inside my head again.

Suddenly the pain of my blisters is obliterated by a wave of guilt that hits me. I shake my head to clear my thoughts, but it is another minute before I can focus on moving my hands back to the first aid kit.

"Thanks, Lucas," I whisper as I rip open an alcohol prep pad.

I wipe the blade with alcohol to sterilize it, then swiftly draw it across my blisters. Clear pus oozes out. I squeeze the bulbs of liquid until the blisters have drained, then wrap them tightly with the Band-Aids.

My foot taken care of, it's time to get dressed. I pull a sweat-stained T-shirt over my head, then a thin long-sleeve shirt.

My raincoat goes on next. "Always dress in layers," Lucas's dad had told me when I had first started camping with them. "Layers let you regulate your temperature. One of the most common things to deal with on the trail is hypothermia, and you can get it by both over- and underdressing. If you don't wear enough, your body's going to cool down. If you wear too much, you're going to soak your clothes in sweat, and they'll be useless if the wind picks up or the temperature drops."

I pick up a pair of lightweight hiking pants and slide them on. They are another lesson from Lucas after the two of us had gotten caught in the rain during a camping trip. I had been wearing jeans and they had stuck to my legs like warmth-sucking leeches, making me completely miserable.

"Cotton kills," Lucas had said, echoing his dad's advice. He told me that when it gets wet, it gets heavy and loses its ability to keep you warm. After that trip, Lucas had given me a pair of his old nylon hiking pants. I never had to wait long for them to dry.

Everything I was doing that morning was reminding me of Lucas.

CHAPTER 4

LAST SUMMER, LUCAS and I made the List.

It was the weekend after school had let out, and the two of us were in the middle of our Saturday morning ritual of gobbling down breakfast in my kitchen. Gran had left a thick stack of pancakes for us to eat before heading into town to run errands.

"You know," said Lucas, stuffing an entire pancake in his mouth, "weshldwridownsmthgs."

"Huh?" I asked, slathering butter on five pancakes before pouring syrup over them.

Lucas took a big gulp of juice. "We should write down some things. A list of all the totally awesome things we want to do this summer."

I sliced into my stack and forked a huge chunk of pancake into my mouth. "How about we put 'Eat twenty pancakes in one sitting' at the top?" I mumbled.

"We basically do that every Saturday," Lucas said, waving away my idea. He got a pen and piece of paper from a kitchen drawer. "We should do something new. What about fishing?"

"Sure!" I liked how the list was starting out already. Fishing was easy. And safe.

By the end of the breakfast we had written the following:

#1: Go fishing
#2: Eat a worm
#3: Spend a whole day at the movie theater
#4: Build a tree house
#5: Go blueberry picking
#6: Make a raft and float it
#7: Explore the abandoned house on Chimney Hill
#8: Learn how to pop wheelies on our bikes

I mopped my last bite of pancake over my syrup-sticky plate and got up to clear the table. I was nearly at the sink when Lucas asked the question.

"Why don't we put 'Jump off the rope swing at the quarry' on the list?"

The plate slipped from my fingers and shattered on the floor.

I hated that note of excitement in Lucas's voice. It always came out when he wanted to do something risky. He was the brave one, chasing adventure wherever it went. I would follow him, but half the time I would mess up somehow. Forget to bring something or do something. Then depend on Lucas to figure out how to save us from my dumb mistakes. Ever since the car accident, I hadn't been able to shake the feeling that bad luck followed me wherever I went. I was the cursed kid whose own parents didn't even want him.

"I don't know." I pictured the rope swing, dangling at least twenty feet above the water. Every summer we watched the older kids doing it, shrieking as they leaped. I'd never thought about doing it myself.

"We're starting middle school this fall. Don't be so chicken. It'll be fun."

Suddenly the desire to be as brave as Lucas surged past my fear. "All right," I said.

Lucas wrote it down as I swept the pieces of my broken plate into a dustpan and into the trash.

#9: Jump off the rope swing at the quarry

"We need one more thing to make it an even ten. Let's make it something big, Toe."

Toe was the nickname Lucas had given me last summer when a Godzilla of a bee had buried its stinger into my big toe. It's one syllable short of my real name, Toby. Lucas only used Toe when he was talking about something really important.

I put the dustpan away and crossed the kitchen to Lucas, leaning over his shoulder to look at the list. An idea popped into my head. "You know how we like to hike?"

Lucas nodded, the pen still poised above the paper. "Mm-hmm."

"How about we hike the tallest mountain we can get to?"

A slow grin filled Lucas's face. "I have a better idea. Why don't we hike the whole Appalachian Trail?"

My hands fell onto the back of Lucas's chair. I was glad I wasn't holding anything that could break. "The entire thing? Isn't it two thousand miles long or something?"

"Let me look it up." Lucas took out his phone and began tapping away. "Two thousand one hundred ninety miles, to be exact," he announced, his face falling. "That's at least a thousand miles too much for me." He bent over the phone, his thumbs swirling rapidly. "Hang on, I've got another idea." He held up his phone and waved it around. "Look at this."

I looked at the phone. There were names of places, with little mile indicators next to them.

"I found a website that shows the distances between shelters on the trail. You know that one that's just a mile from your backyard?"

I nodded. Velvet Rocks Shelter was an easy walk from my yard. Gran and I sometimes had picnics there.

"Well, it's four-hundred forty miles from Velvet Rocks Shelter to Mount Katahdin at the end of the trail in Maine. If we hike ten miles a day, we could finish the whole trail in a month and a half, easy. We could do it before school starts!" Lucas was nodding to himself, excited. "I'll ask my dad if he can come with us. He's been talking about doing a long hiking trip for a while." He picked up the pen and added:

#10: Hike the Appalachian Trail from Velvet Rocks to Katahdin

And that was the List.

CHAPTER 5

I TUCK MY memories into the back of my mind and unzip the tent flap to face the day.

"Aaaaahhh," I sigh. Taking a whiz in the morning is one of the chiefest pleasures of being out on the trail. You tend to hold it during the night—you don't want to leave the huddled warmth of your sleeping bag, you don't want to let in bugs, or zombies, and so usually by daybreak the urge to go is overwhelming.

When I first started camping with Lucas and his dad, one of the first things I discovered was that relieving myself against a tree in the early dawn light is just about the best feeling in the world.

I finish my business and check the sky. The rain clouds are quickly turning leaden gray. I have to get packed and moving—and eat—if I am going to stay warm during the heavier rain.

I make my way to a tall maple tree to get my food. A lumpy sack dangles from a branch fifteen feet up. Hanging your food keeps it out of reach of *all* general wildlife, but the sack you use is generally called a bear bag. I guess "squirrel bag" or "mouse bag" doesn't sound all that protective.

The bear bag is attached to a line of rope that I've coiled around the trunk of the maple. I undo the rope, and the bag falls to the ground with a light thump. I loosen the nylon cord around the bag's mouth and pull out the contents. I knew there wasn't much food left, but it still makes me nervous to see it: three Snickers bars, a bagel, a quarter block of cheddar cheese, and a small Ziploc full of M&M'S.

I pick out my third-to-last Snickers bar and peel back the wrapper. Gran wouldn't approve, and I'm sure there will be some unhappy dentist visits later, but for now, chocolate and peanuts and caramel are the perfect breakfast.

After wolfing down the Snickers, I jam my belongings into my pack and begin breaking down the tent, shaking drops of water off the rain fly before folding it in half and placing the aluminum tent poles at one end. I roll the tent up to the other end, then stuff it all into the tent bag. I clip the tent to my pack using the two thin outer straps at the pack bottom, then heft everything onto my shoulders.

The last thing I have to do is orient myself in the right direction. I unzip my hip pocket and pull out a Ziploc stuffed with maps. I open the one that shows where I am and where I have to go today. The next shelter is eight miles away.

I shake off the urge to look at the part of the map that shows Velvet Rocks Shelter. Or the unmarked spot a mile west, where Gran lives.

Gran and Velvet Rocks are behind me. I have to focus on what's ahead.

I fold the map back up and shove it into the Ziploc, then cram everything back into my hip pocket. As I pull at the zipper, it gets caught on the Ziploc. I tug harder, sealing the plastic into the teeth. I'll worry about it later. Right now I want to get going.

I hop on the trail and start walking. I'm only a few steps in when my pack straps begin to chafe. It feels like two lines of fire are raging down my chest. The pack had seemed so comfortable when I tried it on at home. But that was before I had filled it with thirty pounds of equipment and supplies. Now, even though calluses have started to form, every time my pack shifts, it still hurts.

I bite my lip and try to take my mind off the pain. I concentrate on the two-by-six-inch white blazes that mark the path. They are like tiny North Stars, leading me up to Maine. As I get into the rhythm of hiking, I start to forget the little pains and lose myself in the woods. Plus, it's comforting to know that with every white splash of paint I spot in the woods, I'm getting closer to fulfilling my promise to Lucas.

I'm feeling pretty good until I come to a river crossing that looks way too familiar. The trail is a lot of trees and more trees, but rivers are more memorable. I frown. I could swear that I've been here before.

I stand at the river's edge and yank at the hip pocket zipper. Oh yeah, still stuck. Frustrated, I yank harder and slowly force the pocket open. As I take out the Ziploc, I groan. The zipper has chewed a gaping hole on the corner. So much for my waterproof map bag.

I dig up the map that I need. It confirms my fears. I wasn't supposed to come to a river crossing for miles. I've been following the trail, but in the completely wrong direction. Like a total moron, I literally exited my campsite and started walking back in the direction I'd come from.

Of course I messed up. I always do. I shove the map back into the ruined bag and try to zip the pocket shut. But no matter how hard I pull, it's stuck for real this time. Great.

I snatch the Ziploc out of the broken hip pocket and shrug off my pack. I kneel down and open the hood, but it's too full to fit the maps. I take out my water filter and set it down so I can push the maps inside. As I put the maps into the hood pocket, the filter rolls into the water.

"No!" I drop everything and grab at the filter. I miss. I chase it down the river and nearly swipe it half a dozen times, but then a burst of wind pushes the filter into fast, deep water, and it is lost.

I grit my teeth and return to my pack just in time to see another gust of wind pick up my map bag and toss it into the current. Before I can blink, the ragged Ziploc sails into the water and tumbles away.

Typical. It's just my rotten luck. My stupid, rotten luck. Now I'm going to have to really make sure that I'm going in the right direction.

It takes me a long time to get back to where I had camped the night before. I trudge past it, kicking a clod of dirt and rock toward my old tentsite. I hate making mistakes. But they seem to find me wherever I go.

I continue on, plodding up to a flat, bald peak as fat drops of rain begin to fall. My backpack slumps against my shoulders. I can feel my bruise throbbing under the shoulder strap. It hurts. When I reach the top of the mountain, there is no view. Just cold mist and clouds and a trail sign in all caps: "THIS TRAIL IS EXTREMELY TOUGH. IF YOU LACK EXPERIENCE PLEASE USE ANOTHER TRAIL. TAKE SPECIAL CARE AT THE CASCADES TO AVOID TRAGIC RESULTS."

"That's me," I mutter. "Just a tragic result waiting to happen."

But I keep going anyway.

The trail descends for a long stretch, and as the rain starts to fall harder I realize that I'm starting to get chilly. The first keep on my list needs attention.

I stop for a round of jumping jacks. Hands up, hands down. Legs out, legs in. Repeat. After a minute I feel it—the bumping of my heart against my rib cage. When I shove my hands back into my raincoat, they are warmer.

I continue down from the peak into a forest of thick, gnarled trees. Moss hangs like beards off their branches. Roots twist up, octopus-like, catching my feet as I go by.

It is quiet here. No birds are chirping, and despite the lush growth of ferns and lichens and the steady dripping of rainwater on the green summer leaves, it's too still. It feels like an abandoned jungle, as if all the animals have fled from some awful presence.

A gust of wind blasts through the trees, and the rain changes its tune. Before, it was a drumbeat. Now it is a hammer, beating down with relentless fury.

This is no longer a morning drizzle—this is a storm. I pick up the pace. There are lean-tos, sturdy three-sided log shelters, every couple of miles along the trail. I need to get to the next one to wait out the rain.

The wind begins to howl. Branches crack, and frantic leaves spin through the air. The clouds are black with rain. Thunder growls over my head, and even though I don't see it, I hear the explosion of lightning hitting somewhere above the tree line.

Up until now, I've been so focused on taking care of my keeps list that I haven't paused to think about the bigger picture. But suddenly I'm aware of how alone I am. With the rough terrain and nasty weather, every stumble on a slick rock could turn into a fall. Every step could be a sprained ankle or a broken leg.

And I've violated the number one rule of hiking. I have told no one where I am. Not even Gran. If I get hurt or lost, no one will come looking for me.

I could die out here in these woods.

Cold creeps through my veins. And it's not just the weather seeping into my bones. I am scared. What am I doing out here, without Lucas? It was stupid of me to think that I could survive the trail without him.

Lucas was the leader of our two-kid pack, the one who always knew what to do. I was the happy-to-follow sheep. Now I'm alone, in the middle of a violent storm, rain pelting down, shivering and almost out of food.

Stupid, stupid, stupid.

My heart is racing with fear, and without thinking, I begin to run. My boots splash through puddles, soaking my calves with muddy water. I clench and unclench the straps of my backpack, trying to keep my numb hands from freezing. Chunks of wet hair glue themselves to my forehead.

The trail stretches on, seemingly endless as I stumble forward, pausing just once to put on all my clothes and gulp down the bagel and the rest of my M&M'S. Despite these precautions, I am cold and growing colder. Shivers spasm through my body, becoming more and more uncontrollable.

My keeps list has gone out the window—I can't keep warm; I can't keep fed; I can't keep an eye on the nonexistent sun. And in the cold, damp wetness, I realize I have forgotten to keep hydrated.

I lose track of time. My teeth are knocking together so hard I can feel my brain bouncing around in my head. The rain is still coming down and now the wind has picked up, blowing deep, numbing cold through my jacket. Everything is wet. I have given up on trying to feel my fingers or my toes.

A twisted oak root rises up across the trail, and before I can react, I have caught my foot on it and gone sprawling. I hit the ground hard, breaking the fall with my arms, but my face is inches from a rock.

My backpack presses down on me, and my cheek falls onto the cold stone.

I am tired. I've barely begun, and I already want to give up. I let myself sink into the wet ground. "I'm sorry, Lucas," I whisper. I close my eyes, trying to block out my grief. I've failed my best friend.

And then there is a hand on my shoulder. I turn my head and, in the drizzling rain, a face comes into focus.

"Hey. Hey, kid! You okay?"

I'm too tired to shake my head. The next thing I know, I'm being picked up, backpack and all, and carried. Right before I pass out I see it. Ahead, on the trail. A stack of logs covered by an old tin roof.

Shelter.

CHAPTER 6

IT HAS STOPPED raining by the time I wake. Late-afternoon light shuffles through the patchy clouds and into the shelter where I am lying. I hear the sound of murmuring voices. Two teenage guys are sitting in the shelter, huddled around the flickering blue flames of their stove. A pot sits on top, simmering with water.

One guy has a mess of curly black hair poking out from underneath a dark-blue bandanna. A two-inch scar cuts across his cheek, stopping just shy of his left nostril. His mouth tightens into a thin line as he lifts the pot to pour hot water into a tall metal thermos.

The other wears a bright-blue ball cap that matches his eyes. The cap has a stick figure paddling a canoe and "Life is Good" embroidered across the front in script. He turns off the stove and reaches into his jacket, pulling out several packets of Swiss Miss.

Both of them are decked out in high-tech gear— Arc'teryx hardshells, Patagonia pants, Outdoor Research gloves and gaiters. Gleaming Black Diamond trekking poles rest against brand-new Osprey packs bulging with supplies. The only difference is, Bandanna Dude wears nothing but black, while Ball Cap Guy is dressed in blue.

These guys are not much older than me, but their confidence and expensive-looking gear make them seem way more experienced. They look like the kind of kids Lucas and I would watch jumping into the quarry.

I am still wet but, miraculously, not frozen. My soaked rain jacket lies next to my head. I look down and see a flash of silver. I have been wrapped like a burrito in an emergency blanket. It's made of thin, foil-like Mylar that's supposed to reflect 90 percent of the heat you generate back onto you. On top of that, an unfamiliar sleeping bag is piled over my body. The blanket crinkles like Christmas wrapping paper as I sit up.

"He's awake." The guy with the ball cap picks up a cup and pours hot water into it. He comes over to me and kneels down. He tears open a packet of Swiss Miss. I get dizzy from the smell of powdered chocolate.

Ball Cap pours the Swiss Miss into the cup and stirs it with a blue plastic spork. "Here you go," he says.

I cradle the cup and let the hot steam warm my face. I'm afraid my first sip will scorch my tongue, but the boiling pot water has been mixed with some cold water, and the temperature is just right. Tiny marshmallows float on top like heavenly little clouds. It is the best hot chocolate I have ever had.

I try to make it last, but it takes only thirty seconds before I drain everything. "Thanks," I say to Ball Cap. His blue eyes twinkle as I lick the ring of melted white fluff below the cup's edge. "The marshmallows made that just right."

"No problem." The guy takes back the cup. "I'll get you a refill. By the way, the name is Denver." He nods over to Bandanna Dude, who has not budged an inch from the stove. "And that's Sean."

"I'm To—Tony."

Sean snorts. "Totony?"

"I mean, Tony." If these two boys recognize my name, it might be the end of the trail for me. I told Gran not to worry, but I wouldn't put it past her to have plastered all of New Hampshire with missing posters of me by now.

Denver gives me a second cup of chocolate. This time, I'm able to stretch it out to a full minute.

"Do you want any food? We've got plenty." Denver unzips the top pocket of his backpack and digs out a ham-and-cheese sandwich. I accept it gratefully.

Sean stares at me from across the shelter. "You were a mess out there. And why are you hiking alone? You clearly can't take care of yourself."

I can feel him sizing me up. A dripping-wet kid in the rain who barely made it to shelter before collapsing of hypothermia. Alone and unprepared, probably needing help with each step until he finally gets off the trail. Sean's eyes flicker. I can feel his annoyance. Already I have become a burden to him.

I make up an answer fast. "I'm getting my advanced Wilderness Survival badge for Boy Scouts. I have to spend a week in the woods on my own." I pray that Sean and Denver have never done Boy Scouts. A week in the woods was definitely not a requirement for the badge.

"Well, you're doing a lousy job at earning that badge." Sean shrugs and sips from his thermos.

I reluctantly push the sleeping bag and emergency blanket off me. Curls of body steam escape from my damp clothes. I shiver. "Thanks for the chocolate and the sandwich," I tell Denver.

"You heading out now?" Denver takes the sleeping bag and begins stuffing it in his compression sack.

"Yeah. I think I'll try to get to the next shelter." My voice sticks a little, rusty. "It'll be good to have a roof over my head for the night."

Denver nods. "Kinsman Pond? We're going there, too. According to the map, it's four miles away."

"We were aiming for Lonesome Lake Hut, which is only two miles farther on," says Sean. "But you slowed us down."

"Don't worry about that," Denver says, glancing at Sean. "We're in no rush."

"Well, I won't hold you guys up any longer." I reach for my rain jacket and gingerly slide into it. Even soaked, it will protect me from the wind.

"If you want to wait, Sean and I will be packing up soon. You could hike with us." Denver ignores the scowl that Sean gives him.

I want to follow with these guys. I want to feel safe behind their conversation and their well-stocked backpacks.

But from the way Sean is glaring at me, I know he doesn't want to be bothered.

I decide to compromise. "You guys are probably a lot faster than I am. How about I start off now, and I'll see you on the trail whenever you catch up."

Denver nods. "Sounds good."

"Whatever," says Sean.

I put on my backpack and head out, making sure to go the right way this time. The trail turns into a gentle logging trail, then hitches left past tumbling cascades swollen with new rain and inky-black pools. Moss and roots drape themselves over hip-high boulders, forming little dark caverns. It is lush and spooky. A haunting place for angry ghosts.

I'm glad that Denver and Sean are behind me.

As I follow the trail beside the brook, I see a brief rush of dirty matted fur. A fox, I think. And then I see a familiar rib cage. It is the dinner-stealer from last night.

The dog lopes through the brush at least ten yards from the trail. He is keeping his distance. There is no hot pot of spaghetti for him to kick right now. But he knows that I have been generous in the past.

I think about the food I have left. Two Snickers. A quarter block of cheese.

I have to be careful with this decision. If I feed the dog now, he's only going to expect more. He might get aggressive. Plus, I was running low on food when I met him, but now I'm really almost out.

And then I remember Sean saying that Lonesome Lake Hut was two miles from Kinsman Pond Shelter. Doing the math, that's a little over five miles from where I am.

A hut is different from a shelter. They are luxuries in the woods, with bunks and blankets and food during the summer. Eight of them are spaced out across the toughest sections of the White Mountains, with college-age kids running the show. Lucas and I often talked about working in them when we were old enough.

At Lonesome Lake Hut, I would be able to buy food. I have two hundred and forty-three dollars rolled up in a Ziploc and tucked in a hidden pocket on the inside of my hood. It's all the money I've earned from years of mowing lawns and raking yards and odd jobs around town. I'm hoping it's enough to last me to Mount Katahdin.

The Snickers can keep me going for five more miles, I decide. I break out my block of cheese. The dog trots forward. He is hesitant, unsure of what I will do. But this time, he is not going to rush me.

I toss the cheese, and the dog catches and swallows it in one fast gulp. "Sorry, dog, but that's all I've got," I tell him. He seems to understand. As I continue down the trail, he follows me, but he doesn't beg.

"Tony!" I turn back and see Sean and Denver coming up the trail. Sean is in the lead. He spots the bag of bones following me. "Is that your dog?"

"No, but I've been feeding him a little."

"Why?"

I bite back the urge to tell Sean off. "He's pretty hungry."

"But so are you. Back at the shelter, you ate Denver's sandwich in three bites. You can't afford to feed something else if you don't have enough food for yourself."

Sean is right. I don't like it, but he is right. I'm doing what I've always done. Messing up. Making the wrong decision. Giving a dog food when I needed it more. And now he's looking to me for more food and I can't give him anything. He was wrong to trust me.

"C'mon, Sean. Give the kid a break." Denver unzips the hip pocket of his pack and pulls out a granola bar. He unwraps it and tosses it. A snap and a bite, and the granola bar is gone.

The dog scuttles back off the trail. His eyes are on us, wary but hopeful. I can't spare him any more food, but I have a feeling that we're going to have some company over the next few miles.

Sean hitches up his backpack. It is clear that he is impatient. "C'mon, we need to get going."

I fall in line between Sean and Denver, and breathe a sigh of relief. I'm back at my old place—following. Having people take care of me. I know I need to be able to make it on my own, but for now the company feels great.

CHAPTER 7

SEAN FORGES ALONG with a smooth, practiced gait. I fall into the rhythm of his pace, trying to hide my wheezy breathing so he doesn't realize how much effort it's taking me to keep up.

The trail brings us to the edge of a small muddy pond with long grassy weeds growing up from the bottom. "How are you doing on water?" asks Denver.

I pull out my two water bottles and shake them. They rattle with a few stray drops. "I'm nearly empty."

"You need to fill up here—we won't be hitting another water source until the shelter," says Sean.

I kneel down by the pond and open my bottles. I'm about to dip them into the pond when Sean asks, "Hey, how are you going to purify your water? Don't you have a filter or iodine?"

I shake my head. "I lost my filter at a river crossing this morning. I'll just drink straight from the rivers and streams until I can find another one."

"Purifying your water is no joke." Sean folds his arms disapprovingly. "Haven't you heard of giardia?"

He doesn't wait for my response. "It's like this: You come to a little pond. You drink a tiny mouthful of unpurified water. You don't think it can hurt you. But in that water there could be some animal crap. Moose crap. Deer crap. Beaver crap and squirrel crap and owl crap. And in that crap there could be these little balled-up giardia cysts just waiting to hatch."

Sean's voice pitches up a little higher. "And you drink those cysts because you think, 'Just this one time, I'll be okay.' But then the acid in your stomach gets them to hatch into wriggling parasites that attach to the walls of your intestine.

"Then the parasites feed off you, growing and multiplying until there are billions of them, eating you from the inside out. Then they roll up into cysts again and you crap them out in the weeks of diarrhea that you get, along with being so tired you can't get out of bed for weeks and cramps so bad it makes the worst stomachache you've had feel like a fairy tale."

"Sean, we don't have to know every detail." Denver's voice has a note of warning in it.

"No, it's okay. I know giardia's serious." I try to keep my voice steady, but it still comes out shaky. I'm not used to being yelled at, and it makes me a little scared of Sean.

Sean thumps his pack on the ground and pulls out a three-liter CamelBak water bladder.

Bladders sound gross, but they're actually a lot better than bottles, as long as they don't leak. Every time I want to take a drink I have to stop and unload my bottles from my pack. Meanwhile, a bladder has a water hose that snakes up through a hiker's pack and attaches to the front of a shoulder strap. Any time a hiker gets thirsty, all he has to do is chomp on the hose's bite valve without breaking stride.

Sean removes a small black bag with a nylon drawstring from a side pocket on his pack. Opening the bag, he empties out what looks like a tiny fire extinguisher with a pumping handle at the top and two tubes emerging out of one side. He lowers one of the tubes into the pond and places the second tube into the water bladder. "D, keep the tubes steady while I pump."

Denver comes over and holds the tubes in place as Sean suctions dirty pond water into the filter. Clear, clean water flows through the second tube and into the bladder. When it is full, Denver moves the tube over to his own water bladder. Then he fills my water bottles as well.

After filling up, Sean packs away the filter. "Let's get going," he says shortly.

Before we leave, Denver digs into his pack and hold up a bottle of iodine pills. "You know how to use these?"

I shake my head. When I went camping with Lucas, we always used a water filter.

Denver hands me the pills. "Put two in each bottle. Screw the bottle caps back on, but don't close them all the way. In five minutes, wispy brown threads will form under the caps. Shake them loose, then tighten your bottles."

"I don't need all of these." I'm about to open the bottle and take just a few pills, but Denver shakes his head. "Keep it all, Tony. It's our backup. You need it more than us."

"And find a way to get another filter." Sean has already started walking down the trail. "You'll end up in the hospital if you don't."

We leave the pond and wind our way along the green, wet, muddy trail. We've crossed a small real road, beginning a steep climb, when Denver asks, "So, Tony, how long are you out here for?"

I try to sound casual. "Oh, just a couple of days."

"Do you have enough to eat now?" Denver sounds worried.

"I've got two Snickers bars. And some cheese. Wait, no, no cheese. Just the Snickers."

Sean snorts. "What? I knew you were low, but that is borderline stupid. And you fed that dog? Such a newb."

I decide at that moment that I don't like Sean.

Denver pulls up beside me. "Tony, that's not enough. You're going to need more food than that."

"I know. But it's all I've got." I want to let Denver know that I'm not completely dumb, that I do have plans to keep myself from starving. "And once I get to Lonesome Lake, I'll be able to stock up."

Denver opens a hip pocket strap and pulls out a Ziploc bag full of homemade gorp. That stands for "good old raisins and peanuts." Denver's mix has colorful flashes of M&M'S added as well.

Denver seems to be a decent guy, and I feel a momentary pang of unease. I made a decision to hike this trail alone, and I don't want to feel like I owe anyone anything. I don't want to get too involved with these guys.

But he stuffs it into my hand, like it isn't even a question.

I open the Ziploc and pop a handful of peanuts, raisins, and M&M'S in my mouth. I can feel fat and sugar breaking down as I chew. My stomach howls with happy anticipation.

"Hungry, huh?" Denver has a smile on his face. I'm almost angry at him, for thinking friendship could be so easy, for acting like I'm some little kid—but I know he means well.

"Yeah," I mumble, trying not to demolish the entire bag.

"Eat it all—we've got plenty of food for our trip."

I swallow another handful of sweet, free food and gulp down my anger. "How far are you guys going?"

"After Kinsman Pond we're heading up to Franconia Ridge—Liberty, Lafayette, Little Haystack—then over the Presidential Range to Mount Washington. We go down to Pinkham Notch from there. We've got Sean's car parked at the visitor center. We're planning for it to take four days, but we've got enough supplies for five or six."

The names ring bells in my head. Mount Washington for sure. It's the tallest peak in the Northeast, and is said to have some of the worst weather on earth. The Appalachian Trail runs right over it.

▲▲

"And what about you—how far are you planning to go for your week in the woods?" Denver asks.

I am confused until I remember the lie I've told them. About earning my Boy Scouts merit badge. "I don't know yet," I say cautiously. I don't want to let on that I'm planning to hike all the way to Katahdin. "Probably past Washington a little ways—I'll have to see."

Denver doesn't press, and we go along in a comfortable silence. I've just begun to notice the soft rustle of wind through the maples when Denver asks, "So, Tony. How did you get into hiking?"

I don't respond right away. I keep in step with these two guys who clearly are far more prepared than I am, and try not to think about the answer to that question.

It comes to me anyway.

CHAPTER 8

WE HAD DONE almost all the things on the List. Almost every single one. While we were checking things off our list, we were also planning for our big hike. We read up on hiking in the White Mountains of New Hampshire and through the 100 Mile Wilderness in Maine. We made a list of things we would need: sleeping bags, sleeping pads, tent, boots, socks . . . all the way down to cups and first aid kits and maps.

We found water bottles and the MSR cooking stove at one garage sale, Swiss Army knives and a water filter and headlamps from another. There were well-used backpacks in the gear room where Lucas's dad kept all his camping supplies. Lucas had our shelter—an army-green Stansport tent he had gotten from his dad when he was eight.

We planned simple meals. Pasta and sauce, rice and beans, peanut butter and tortillas, ramen noodles. We got maps of the trail and studied them by flashlight in our creaky tree house as lightning bugs darted by, their golden pulses as brief and bright as hope.

The time when I knew that we were going to actually go, though, was when Lucas knocked on my door one Friday night in early July and told me to be ready for a surprise the next morning. "We're going to Boston and we've got to get there early," he announced.

"Is this for the trail?" I asked.

"You'll see." Lucas smiled mysteriously. "Set your alarm for three a.m. and bring as much cash as you can. I promise you, it'll be worth it."

I set my alarm, but it didn't matter. I was up all night, fidgety and excited. By 2:00 a.m. I was out of bed, and by 2:47 a.m. I was tapping at the front door of Lucas's house with three twenties shoved into the back pocket of my jeans.

We got into Lucas's mom's Subaru Legacy and she drove us through town, with its nickel-and-dime store-fronts, past Dan & Whit's general store, which advertises in plain-printed type in their front window, "If we don't have it, you don't need it!" We passed by the redbrick town hall and by the tiny post office where Mr. Dinkins had worked for thirty-six years.

We stayed on Route 5 for a mile before taking the sharp-curved ramp to I-91 south. On the highway, I finally fell asleep to the quiet hum of the car and the lull of the road. I was still dreaming when the digital clock on the Legacy's dash turned to 5:27 a.m. and we pulled into the Landmark Center parking lot.

Lucas nudged me and hopped out of the car. He pointed at a big box store with a line of sleepy customers waiting next to the glass double doors. "Today's the REI's scratch-and-dent sale."

I was suddenly very awake. REI scratch-and-dent sales are like Christmas for anyone who loves the outdoors. They are exactly as advertised—any slightly damaged returned items go on sale a couple of times a year at huge discounts. Sometimes a customer returns something because it's the wrong size, or the wrong color, and that's when you can get a perfect piece of gear at half off or more.

Lucas and I dashed to the end of the line. His mom came more slowly, bringing muffins and a thermos of hot chocolate for us to drink as we waited. When the doors opened at eight, we scampered like rabbits to the camping section. I found a moisture-wicking base layer and some lightweight Darn Tough hiking socks and was looking at a basic first aid kit when Lucas tapped my arm. "Toe, check these out!"

And there they were. Asolo hiking boots, chestnut brown, coated with waterproof Gore-Tex. Two-inch rubber soles. High-quality leather and precise stitching all crafted into one perfect set of boots dangling by their laces from Lucas's hands.

I sat down in the middle of the store and pulled them on. They were stiff, but when I stood up and walked around the store to test them out, I could feel them molding to my feet, as though they were mine already.

Then I looked down at the price tag, and my heart crumbled. Even at the steep discount, there was no way I could shell out that amount of money.

I took them off and handed them back to Lucas. "Man, these are great, but I don't think I can afford them. Thanks for spotting them, though." I picked up the items I had tossed in a heap in my eagerness to try on the boots. "I'll get these. Meet you in the car."

A day later I returned home from a walk with Gran to find a lumpy brown paper package scotched-taped together sitting on the front porch. I ripped open the paper, and the Asolo boots fell out. A note had been stuffed inside one of them. When I unfolded it, there was only one line, written in Lucas's scrawl.

Shut up and don't thank me.

I never did.

CHAPTER 9

LUCAS. I GOT into hiking and I'm on the trail in my muddy Asolo boots because of Lucas and the List.

"Tony? Earth to Tony . . ."

I shake myself out of my memories. It has been a few minutes since Denver asked me why I was on the trail. The silence must have felt strange. It was a straightforward question, after all.

"I got into hiking because I'm trying to grow up." It's the best half truth I can give.

" 'Grow up'?" Ahead of me, Sean shakes his head. "What does that even mean?"

"I've . . . always needed people. I've always been a follower. Out here on the trail, I want to learn how to grow up. Depend on myself. Learn how to be alone." The last answer slips past me before I can catch it.

A bird flutters out of the brush. A quail, I think. Its light-brown body lifts off, and it disappears into the trees.

Sean does not respond, and we spend the next hour in silence, lost in our own thoughts. We pass through muddy trails slick with new rain, up a steep mile to the top of South Kinsman, down a rocky scramble, up again to the peak of North Kinsman, and make it to Kinsman Pond Shelter an hour after all our stomachs have started to growl.

No one else is there, and we take over the shelter, flopping our backpacks into the corner. I think about hiking the extra couple of miles to Lonesome Lake so I can get more food, but I quickly decide against it. After my hypothermia scare earlier today, I don't trust myself to not mess up. Plus, it's getting dark and I don't want to leave the protection of my rescuers.

Sean and Denver break out their cooking equipment and make their dinner, a soupy mess of jasmine rice and plump red kidney beans floating among thick slices of summer sausage, all simmering in a heap of Cajun seasonings. As the stew cooks, the smell is unbearably good.

But when Denver offers to share with me, I say no. Instead, I eat my second-to-last Snickers, forcing myself to chew slowly. I count to twenty for every bite, making each mouthful last as long as possible. I want to prove to Sean that I am taking responsibility for feeding the dog. That I'm not going to depend on luck and the generosity of others to make it on the trail.

It's not enough. The hunger in my belly takes over, and I snatch my final Snickers and rip open the wrapper. It is halfway gone before I can force myself to stop. I clamp my mouth shut and tuck the last half in the top pocket of my backpack. I'm not out of food. I'm not desperate. Yet.

There is no flat place to pitch a tent, and the ground is soggy from the day's rain, so after dinner we all decide to stay in the shelter. We roll out our sleeping pads on the dry wooden floor and fluff up our sleeping bags on top of them. Night comes, and each of us shuffles into our patch of warmth for the night.

It is when we are all inside our bags, breathing the cool summer-night air, and I'm wondering if either Sean or Denver snore, that Sean puts his hands behind his head and studies the roof beams above our heads.

"Hey, Tony," he says. "I've been thinking about what you said. You want to learn how to be alone?" He scratches his neck. "Just give up on everybody."

I am confused. "What do you mean?"

Sean unclasps one of his hands and runs his thumb across his cheek. The moonlight glows against the dark line of his scar. "When you can say *screw you* to everyone, when you can feel them not caring, and not care about them, then you've made it. You're alone. You trust no one but yourself. You look out for no one but yourself. And you survive."

"But what about your family?" I think about Gran. The way she had hugged me so hard after what happened with Lucas, I thought my bones would crack. "Don't you trust them? Don't they look out for you?"

"No," Sean says.

It's only one word, but there is so much venom behind it that I know it's true. "What about your brothers or sisters?"

"Only child."

"Me, too," I say.

"So what? That doesn't make us friends." Sean shifts so his dark eyes reflect back at mine. "And anyway, having siblings doesn't mean you're less alone. Take Denver. His brother, Harry, is a real piece of work."

"Sean, let's not talk about it." For the first time I hear anger in Denver's voice. And something else. Sadness. Fear.

"Fine. I'm going to sleep," Sean says. He turns his back to me.

"But—"

"Shut up, Tony," he growls.

It is quiet. I stare at the moonlit cobwebs as Sean's breathing grows deep and even. I guess I can see what he means. About not trusting anyone.

But I don't want that kind of alone. I want to be able to trust myself and rely on myself, but I want to be able to trust others, too. Being alone is not the same as being lonely.

Just as I'm about to drift off, Denver's sleeping bag rustles. "Hey, Tony. You still awake?"

"Yeah."

"I know Sean can come off as a little harsh. But he's a good guy."

I think about how different Sean and Denver are. I wonder why they're together—Sean's coldness and Denver's friendliness are like night and day. "How'd you become friends?" I ask.

Denver is silent, and I don't think he's going to answer. Then, when I'm just about to close my eyes, he clears his throat. "When I was twelve, my dad caught this scrawny, scraggly kid stealing the garden gnomes off our front porch. But instead of calling the cops, my dad took him into the house and told my mom to make extra for dinner.

"That night I came home to see Sean in the kitchen, scarfing down a huge plate of food. The first thought I had of him was 'Man, that kid is skinny.' You could see his ribs through his shirt. Later, Sean told me that until that night, he hadn't had a real meal in a week.

"Anyway, after dinner my dad told Sean he could stop by anytime for a meal. He soon became a regular at our house.

"I wasn't sure what to think about Sean at first. He was really quiet. Wouldn't touch anything. I think he was scared that he would somehow mess up. That he would prove that a kid from the bad side of town could only be bad.

"When he started inviting Sean over, my dad sat me and my brother, Harry, down. He told us that even though Sean had stolen from us, we had to trust him. 'Trust builds trust,' he said.

"I listened to my father for the most part, but I still wasn't sure about wanting Sean as a friend. Then, one day, I saw him riding down the street on the way to my house. He was on this old, beat-up skateboard. The paint had been worn to nothing, and the wheels were rubbed down almost to their axles. But Sean was double-flipping and high-jumping on that board as if it were a stroll in the park. I asked him to teach me. We ended up meeting at the local skate park almost every day after school. As we spent more time together, I never worried about trusting him again.

"But Harry was a different story. He never liked Sean. When my parents were away and Sean was over, Harry would always tease him about his Walmart jeans and his ragged homemade haircuts. He constantly accused Sean of wanting to steal our Xbox or PlayStation or whatever new toy we got for Christmas or our birthdays.

"And he wouldn't let up about Sean's shirts. Sean was always wearing long-sleeved shirts, even in summer. They were the really cheap kind, the ones you get in three-packs at the dollar store. Harry would ask Sean why he didn't have T-shirts like a normal person, but Sean just wouldn't answer.

"I couldn't figure it out, until this one really hot day in August. It was about a year after I met Sean. Harry and I were horsing around in the pool in our backyard. Sean was with us but refused to go swimming. Said he was afraid of the water.

"Harry and I got into a wrestling match. Harry has always been stronger than me and liked to prove it, especially if there was an audience. He would hold me under and then lift my head up only enough to get a half breath in before jerking me down back into the water. Each time he dunked me, he held me under for longer. Then he finally got to the point where he wouldn't let me up.

"Later, Sean told me that he had seen my eyes bulge and my mouth open and take in water, and he had screamed to Harry to let go. Instead of pulling me up, Harry had taunted him. Had told him that he was a wuss for not trying to save me. I couldn't hear. I was too busy drowning.

"Sean jumped in. He still had his sneakers on. He really didn't know how to swim. But he could kick and bite, and that's what he did. Harry has a scar from where Sean left teeth marks on his arm.

"Harry let go of me. I got to the surface and pulled myself from the water, choking out half the pool. Harry and Sean were thrashing around in the shallow end. Harry was screaming at Sean that he was fighting dirty, and Sean was screaming back that Harry was a bully and a coward.

"Harry dragged himself out of the pool. He called us horrible names and went inside to take care of his bleeding arm.

"After a while, Sean and I went inside, too. I took Sean to my room and gave him some dry clothes. I went into the bathroom to change, and it occurred to me that Sean didn't have a towel to dry off. I got one from the bathroom shelf and opened my bedroom door.

"Sean was in the middle of dressing. His shirt was off and he was facing away from me. His back and arms were covered in bruises and welts. And not the kind you get from falling off a skateboard.

"Sean had heard the door open. He knew I was behind him.

" 'Don't tell,' he had said.

" 'I won't,' I said. 'But you have to.'

"I handed him the towel and Sean covered himself. He began to shake. We sat on the floor and he told me about his father. About the alcohol, the drugs, and the violence that happened in his home. About the threats of what would happen if he told anyone.

"I didn't know what to do. But I knew someone who would. That night, after supper, I got my dad and Sean in the living room. I got Sean to talk. My dad called Child Protective Services that night, and a week later, Sean was living with us. And a few months later, I was teaching him how to swim."

A loon calls out in the night. It is a lonely, mournful sound. After a while, Denver begins to snore.

I tuck my head down and close my eyes. I still don't like Sean much. But I don't mind his meanness anymore.

CHAPTER 10

HUNGER WAKES ME. My stomach feels like it has shrunk to the size of a robin's egg; it's searching for any last bits of food so it can expand again.

In the gray dawn light, I unscrew my water bottle and take a gulp, then another, hoping to quiet my growling stomach. I unpeel the last bit of wrapper on the last half of my last Snickers bar. This time, I hold each bite and count to fifty.

"Morning, Tony." Denver is pouring hot water into a bowl at the other end of the shelter. The smell of oatmeal hits my nose, thick and rich with brown sugar and cinnamon.

I have to leave immediately, or I'm going to pounce on Denver's breakfast. "Morning." I crumple my Snickers wrapper into my empty bear bag and shove it into my pack, along with everything else. "I'm going to hit the trail early."

"Sounds good." Denver holds a spoonful of oatmeal to his mouth and blows. I can barely look at him. "But when you get to Lonesome, wait up for us. The next stretch of trail is going to be pretty tough, and you shouldn't be doing it alone."

Sean looks up from stuffing his mouth with a peanut-butter-covered bagel. "Denver! We're not dragging this kid with us for our entire trip!"

"Sean. Chill out." Denver glares at his friend.

"Fine. If he can keep up, he can stay with us. But if not, we're ditching him." Sean takes another bite of his bagel and turns his back to me.

I try not to let Sean get to me. "See you guys," I say as casually as I can, and head out.

Lonesome Lake. Lonesome Lake. Lonesome Lake. I match the name of the place with food to the beat of my hunger pangs. I have given up looking at the forest around me. All I want to do is eat.

I start thinking of the delicious things Gran would make for me. Homemade waffles, hot from the waffle iron, covered in strawberries and whipped cream and drizzled with Hershey's chocolate syrup. Lasagna, with its layers of wide noodles and soft ricotta and beefy tomato sauce, covered in melty, bubbling mozzarella. A whole roast chicken, with brown-crisped skin, sliced into long tender pieces and eaten with smooth heaps of buttery mashed potatoes. Apple pie, still warm, served with a wedge of cheddar cheese and a tall glass of milk.

Gran. A pang of guilt shoots through me. I think about the letter I wrote her the night before leaving for the trail, hunching over a piece of loose leaf, biting my pen so hard between every couple of words that the plastic shell broke before I was done.

Gran,
 You have always been there for me. When Mom and Dad left me at the hospital, you stayed and held my hand and kept me safe. After what happened with me and Lucas, when I just wanted to hide from the world forever, you made sure I got out of bed every morning. You made me brush my teeth and eat my breakfast and face the day. You are awesome and I love you.
 But I have to go away. I know you probably know where I'm heading, but please don't come searching for me. I need to be by myself for a while.
 Don't worry—I'll be back before school starts. I promise.
 But I need to do something first.
 Love,
 Toby

I had placed the note on the kitchen table the next morning when she was out on her weekly errand run, knowing that she wouldn't be back for hours. Then I had put on my pack and headed for the trail.

Now I am staring at my feet, pushing one foot in front of the other, thinking about food and Gran and trying so hard not to collapse that I barely notice anything until the silver glimmer of Lonesome Lake comes flashing through the trees.

Then I look up, and I see a dash of movement out of the corner of my eye. Four legs, a familiar scruff. Ratty fur as gnarled as a bird's nest.

It's the dog. He is uncertain, skittering forward two steps, then hopping back one.

I stop and unsling my pack to look half as intimidating. Slowly I bend my knees until I am level with him. A soft, clumsy whistle comes through my mouth. My hand stretches out, open palmed. "Here, boy," I say.

The dog's nose quivers. He is suspicious. If the only kindness he has received is food, then an empty hand must mean something bad.

I keep my hand still. "Hey. I'm not going to hurt you. But I don't have any food left."

I am talking to a dog. It feels natural and good. I push my hand out a tiny bit more.

Long seconds pass. My thighs are burning and my knees start to jiggle back and forth. But I keep my hand steady.

The dog comes. His wet nose brushes my fingers and he licks the palm of my hand. He must have found a smudge of food because he keeps on licking. But he does not bite.

My heart jumps with a fierce kind of joy. For the first time in my life, I feel needed. This dog has eaten my spaghetti supper and my block of cheese, and now he's looking to me for help. I reach down to pet his head.

Instantly the dog is crouched backward with his lips arched, a low growl in his throat. I can see his yellow-stained teeth, the dark pink of his inner cheeks. He's telling me with every bristling hair that he doesn't want to be touched.

I feel a pang of hurt. He doesn't trust me yet.

And then I stand and turn around and the dog is still growling and now I see why.

Fifty feet away, its hooves sinking in the soft mud of the trail, is a moose.

I have only a moment to take in the size of the animal— its chest bigger than a raging full-grown bull—before its massive shoulders tighten. It lowers its head and paws the ground.

I turn to run, and a calf with gangly legs stumbles out from the bushes onto the trail. I had been concentrating so hard on making the dog my friend that I hadn't noticed that I had gotten in between a mama moose and her baby.

If I run toward the calf, the mama will think I'm attacking it. If I run toward the mama, I will be heading straight into a beast with horrible eyesight and a blind desire to trample whatever may be harming her baby.

The mama moose snorts. Her long, narrow ears flatten backward and she lowers her head. She doesn't have antlers but doesn't need any for me to be squashed like a grape.

A charging moose. It's a big thing. And a bad one.

The mama moose starts galloping toward me. I scream at myself to get out of the way, but suddenly I am back in the car that hurtled me toward Lucas, with the rise of the other moose's body rocketing toward the window by my head. I hear the sounds of glass shattering and sirens wailing, and then I see me and Lucas in the hospital and the bright white of our new casts. I know I have to move, but my boots are pinned to the dirt.

There is a blur of dirty fur, and the dog hurtles out from behind me. He plants himself directly in front of my scared, shaking body and barks three times, loud and low.

The moose thunders toward us. As she nears, the dog leaps up, nipping at her broad chest. She swerves to avoid him and crashes into the underbrush off the trail. She does not slow down as she heads toward her baby, and as she passes, I take in the short coarse hairs on her side, the dark scabs around her knees, the sloping hump of her neck, her powerful jaw muscles bulging, her wild smell of swamp and mountains.

And then she is past me and with her calf, and they both go running down the trail toward the lake.

The dog trots back to me. This time, when I put my hand out, he nuzzles his head under it.

"Good dog," I say. The words don't feel like they're enough. It feels strange, not to have a name for an animal that saved your life. I scratch behind his ears and look him full on in the face. "You know what? Your name is Moose from now on. I promise to take care of you. And when we get to Lonesome Lake Hut, you're going to have a feast like you never had before."

CHAPTER 11

A FEW MINUTES later, Lonesome Lake Hut comes into view. Weathered shingles cover the sides and a hodgepodge of tin chimneys and solar panels stick out from the green metal roofing. There's a wraparound wooden deck that overlooks a patch of trees and the lake below. An unbearably wonderful smell of pancakes hovers in the air.

I scratch Moose under the chin and tell him to stay outside before climbing the hut steps and pushing open the door. I want to be quick. If Gran did report me as missing, I don't want anyone to see my face long enough to make the connection.

I've been on the trail for less than a week, but it still comes as a shock to be back indoors. Going inside of Lonesome Lake Hut is like being hugged by civilization. The temperature is warm and cozy. Tall windows let the sunlight in but keep the wind out.

The first things to greet me are long wooden tables with benches tucked neatly underneath them. A chalkboard announces the name of the crew working in the hut as well as the dinner menu for the night—anadama bread, split-pea soup, beef tips, couscous, steamed veggies, and a surprise dessert.

A wooden counter with a stainless-steel top and three sinks divides half the eating area from the kitchen; a sales counter divides the other half. The sales counter is full of stuff to buy—extra socks, headlamps, AA batteries displayed in a glass case at knee level. Appalachian Mountain Club T-shirts for sale hang from a clothesline above.

A fully stocked kitchen lies behind the counters. The wooden shelves are lined with plastic spice containers, full of cumin, cinnamon, curry powder, bay leaves, rosemary, thyme, sage, parsley, basil, and onion and garlic powder. Gallon jugs of molasses, oil, and barbecue sauce rest on the windowpanes. White plastic rolling bins have been wheeled under a stainless-steel table. Traces of flour and oats dust their lids. Five-gallon pots hang from metal hooks dangling from the ceiling.

A guy with wiry brown hair and a scruffy beard stands in front of a six-burner stove, unloading a heap of chopped onions into a soup pot so big, a baby could swim around in it. He's got on a light-green T-shirt with the white blocky outline of a spruce tree across the front. His Carhartt workpants are stained with paint and dirt, and his feet are covered with bright orange Crocs over a pair of thick wool socks.

If Lucas and his dad were here, they'd already be chatting with this guy, asking him what's for dinner, how he likes working in the huts, what his favorite color is. I'd be in the background, waiting until they were done talking so I could have Lucas to myself.

But they aren't here, and I have to talk to this guy if I'm going to get supplies from the hut. I'm about to ask where to get something to eat when I spot them. Lying like open treasure chests on top of the sales counter. Boxes of energy bars with their cardboard lids peeled back. Clif Bars, Luna bars, PowerBars, KIND bars. Flavors that sound like angels have been in the kitchen: chocolate chip peanut crunch, chocolate almond fudge, chocolate-dipped coconut, dark chocolate cherry cashew, peanut butter chunk chocolate.

And there are Snickers bars. Oh, there they are. Lovely Snickers bars.

I feel like a half-starved bear stumbling out of hibernation as I approach the counter, wobbly kneed and achy stomached. I set my pack down slowly. I'm so close to food that I'm trembling, and I'm worried that if I'm not careful I'll lose it and start cramming energy bars in my mouth, wrappers and all. I unzip the top of my pack and find the Ziploc with the rolled-up twenties.

The guy in the kitchen sees me unpeeling a twenty and comes over. "Hi there. What can I get you?"

I hand him the bill and reach for the closest box. I take out a chocolate almond fudge Clif Bar. My hands shake as I make a diagonal tear down the wrapper. The inside foil glints in the sunlight as I raise the bar to my lips and take a bite.

Sugar and chocolate flood my mouth. Before I can stop myself, I am ripping off huge chunks of the bar and swallowing them so fast I stop breathing. The whole thing is gone in about ten seconds. I am dizzy with happiness.

The guy has my twenty, but he seems to have forgotten that he's holding it. "When was the last time you ate?" he asks.

"I had half a Snickers bar this morning," I mumble. I don't want to tell him that I've completely run out of food.

The guy leaves the twenty on the counter. He walks over to the sinks and pulls a rack of dishes out from under them. He takes out a plate, removes a fork and a knife from a silverware holder, and hands them to me. "Sounds like you'll be needing breakfast, then." He points to a shallow pan with a lid over it on one of the long dining room tables. "Pancakes are over there. Have as many as you want."

I wanted to get supplies and get out, but the promise of more food is too powerful. I go over to the pan and slide off the lid. There are at least two dozen fluffy pancakes nestled inside, each as big as my hand. "Thank you, s-s-sir," I stutter.

The guy laughs. "You can call me Andy."

I pull the bench back and set myself down next to the pan, spear half a dozen of the pancakes on my plate, and begin to stuff them whole inside my mouth. I don't need the knife.

Andy comes over with a bottle of maple syrup. It's not the fake kind that they normally serve in the huts because people use so much of it—it's Maine-made honest-to-goodness real maple syrup that he must have gotten from the crew's personal stash. He also brings a full stick of butter.

"Here you go," he says as he sets them on the table. "I'm making you some eggs, too." He goes back to the kitchen and takes a cast-iron skillet down from a hanging hook. A few moments later I hear the hiss and sizzle of frying eggs. "Do you eat meat?" he calls.

"Mm-hmm," I answer.

I've gone through about a dozen pancakes when Andy sets down a second plate in front of me. There are three fried eggs and six sausage links on it, plus a toasted sesame bagel piled high with cream cheese and slices of avocado. "This here's what we like to call hiker's delight," he tells me.

"Thank—"

"Just eat," he says.

I have gobbled down the eggs and half the avocado bagel before I remember. I take my plate and go outside. One by one, I toss the sausage links to Moose, ignoring the urge to save one for myself. I give him my other bagel half, too. Moose snaps everything up in a few gulps.

We are fed. We are full. We are doing all right.

CHAPTER 12

WHEN I GO back inside, Andy is in the kitchen pouring a can of tomato puree into the soup pot. He comes up to the counter when he sees me. I pass him my dirty plate. I figure my breakfast will cost a fortune, but it was worth it. "How much do I owe you?"

"Two bucks for the Clif Bar. Nothing for everything else." Andy hands me eighteen dollars, change for my twenty.

"No." I am determined not to owe him. I give him a ten back. He waves it away, so I shove it into a tip jar on the counter.

Andy sighs and leans his head toward the front windows. "Looks like your friend enjoyed the sausages."

Andy seems like the kind of person who wouldn't gossip about stray kids in huts. I decide to open up to him a little. "I've been giving him what I can. He doesn't have an owner and has been following me since the Kinsmans."

"You can feed him what's left of the pancakes. And I have some dog treats that a hiker left here last week. Take them, too."

Andy takes a box of Milk-Bone biscuits off one of the shelves and hands it to me. This act of kindness almost breaks me. After nearly giving up on the trail yesterday in the miserable pelting rain, too many things are going right. I haven't had this much stuff work out for me. Ever.

I can feel tears welling up. I jerk around and scrub my eyes, hoping that Andy hasn't seen. When I turn back around, Andy is staring at me. He has a curious look on his face. "How far are you planning to hike, kid?" he asks.

I decide to tell him the truth and hope that Sean and Denver don't compare stories with him. "I plan to go straight through the White Mountains and on to Katahdin."

"That's a far ways. You traveling with anybody?"

I nearly tell him that it's just me. Then I think about how weird that would sound. A young kid hiking hundreds of miles by himself. "I'm hiking with my dad, but he's real slow. I don't think he'll be here for another hour at least." I swallow hard. The lie is a lump in my throat. My face is turning hot. I hope Andy doesn't notice.

"Think you and your dad are going to make it?" he asks.

"I've—We've got to."

"And why is that?"

I think about the List. About the way Lucas would cup his hands over a newly lit fire to keep the small flames burning. About promises I have made. I look the guy square in the eye. "I've just got to." My voice is steel.

The hut goes still for a moment.

I expect Andy to poke further, to ask more questions that

I have to make more lies for. Instead, he folds his arms. "Wait here," he says. He disappears down a corridor past a sign that reads "Croo Only." When he comes back, he is holding a glass marble between his thumb and forefinger. It is perfectly clear except for a ribbon of blue swirled through the center.

"This belonged to my great-grandfather." Andy tosses the marble in the air. It winks in the sunlight before disappearing back into his hand. "He was a fighter pilot during World War II. Before he went to war, his five-year-old son gave him this marble. Told him it would keep him safe.

"Not a lot of pilots survived Nazi artillery, but my great-grandfather did. He kept the marble tucked in a special pocket he sewed onto his uniform. At the end of the war, he gave the lucky marble back to his son, who gave it to his daughter, who gave it to her eldest son." Andy taps the marble against his chest. "Me." He holds the marble out to me. "This is for you. You've got a long way ahead of you, and a little luck wouldn't hurt."

"No." The word tumbles out of my throat. I don't deserve this generosity. This faith and trust in me, when I barely have faith in myself.

Andy folds his arms. "I'm not telling you that you can keep it. When you reach Carter Notch Hut, give the marble to the crew. They'll get it back to me. But you look like you could use some help. At least take it through the huts."

I think about it. All my life I've done nothing but screw up. It wouldn't hurt to have something lucky to balance out all the bad luck that weighs my every step.

I hold out my hand. Andy drops the marble into my palm. It is small but surprisingly heavy. Then he goes to the front counter and begins taking Clif Bars and PowerBars out of their boxes. "Open your pack. You've got a ways to go, and you'll be needing supplies."

Half an hour later, my pack is ten pounds heavier and I have one hundred and ninety one dollars remaining in my money Ziploc. Andy has stuffed in boxes of Annie's macaroni and cheese, a dozen instant oatmeal packets, Gatorade mix, a two-pound block of cheese, a jar of peanut butter, three plump summer sausages, and about twenty energy bars. It should be more than enough to get me and Moose through the next couple of days.

I'm tempted to buy a water filter, but the one in the display case is almost a hundred bucks. It's way more than I can afford, so I figure I'll fill up on water in the huts. Plus, Denver's iodine pills should last me a good chunk of the trail into Maine.

And most important, tucked in my hood pocket is a Ziploc sandwich bag with a square of glossy paper detailing all the trails and contour lines of the White Mountains folded inside. I've got a map again.

CHAPTER 13

I AM OUTSIDE, feeding handfuls of dog biscuits to Moose, when Sean and Denver come down the trail. I say hello, and they go inside to have lunch. Moose and I head to the lake, where I avoid families of hikers and find a deserted patch of shore. I skip stones over the calm water while Moose snuffles around the reeds.

When I run out of smooth, flat stones, I sit on the rocky shore and think about the last time I had felt this peaceful by the water. It was the day when Lucas and I had officially gone about tackling the List.

It was only a week after that fateful pancake breakfast. Lucas's dad had strapped the family canoe to the top of the Subaru and had driven us to Lake Winnipesaukee. We'd caught four wriggling trout, and Lucas's dad had scaled and gutted the fish on the picnic table at our campsite. After throwing the scraps to the birds, Lucas and I had rolled the fish in bread crumbs and his dad had panfried them to a crisp golden hue over a roaring campfire.

That night, we had feasted on fresh-caught fish, and as we sat by the lake digesting our meal and watching the stars glitter across the clear night sky, Lucas had pulled out the List and made one long slash across #1: Go fishing. "One down, nine to go," he had said. We had whooped and high-fived our greasy hands.

"Gah!" A sharp prick on the side of my neck brings me out of my daze. I slap at my skin. When I take my hand away, there is a squashed mosquito on my palm, as well as a smear of my blood. My neck is already starting to itch.

I look down and see an army of flies crawling over my pants. Another mosquito lands on my knee and stabs down into my quick-dry pants.

Biting insects are the worst of the bad littles. I bat at my pants, and the flies whirl into my face. I accidentally snort up a bug, but before I can snort it back out, it bullets through my nose and down into my throat. I try not think of how many eyes it has. I decide that I am done with the lake.

I stand up. Moose is waiting for me, his long tail thumping against the rocks. I lean over and scratch him behind the ears. "Hey, buddy."

Moose wiggles his head into my fingers. A stinky pink tongue licks my wrist, and his mouth curls into what I swear is a smile.

I give Moose a final scratch, then head back to the hut. Inside, Sean and Denver are refilling their water bladders in a small silver sink. Andy is nowhere in sight.

"Hey, Tony!" Denver greets me. "You heading out now?"

I nod. "Just got to fill my water bottles and I'll be set." I nervously check the hallway leading to the crew room. If Andy sees me talking with Sean and Denver, he may become suspicious of my story about hiking with my dad.

I hurriedly fill my water bottles and shove them in the side pockets. I sling my pack over my shoulders and nearly fall down. It's a lot heavier than this morning. "Let's go." I am impatient to get out of the hut before Andy reappears.

Sean immediately heads out the door, but Denver waits in the hut until I have clipped my chest and hip straps closed. I stagger out of the hut behind him. We meet up with Sean and get back on our way.

As Denver and Sean stride down the trail, I quickly realize that the only reason that I could keep up with them before was because my pack had weighed half as much as it does now.

As the trail descends, I stumble behind Denver and Sean. My pack straps bite into my shoulders, rubbing them even rawer than before. Every time I lift my foot it's as if I'm sloughing through deep water. I am silently grateful that we are going down instead of up. But even with gravity on my side, the distance between us grows longer and longer. Every once in a while Denver glances behind and waits a few seconds, but Sean does not stop or turn around once. He seems determined to lose me.

After a few miles, the trail comes to a whizzing highway. Up ahead, Denver shouts something to Sean, and he finally stops. He turns and glares at me until I have caught up.

"You're slowing us down," he says sharply. "We've got over nine miles to go before the Garfield Ridge Shelter, and it's already noon. We want to be able to set up camp before dark, but we won't with you hanging on to us like some sort of parasitic tick."

"Easy, Sean," says Denver.

Moose growls. I put my hand on his head to calm him. Sean's words hurt, but he is right. It has been too easy for me to follow them. But I'm not on the trail to be a follower. "You guys go ahead. I'll see you at the shelter."

"Are you sure?" Denver asks.

"Yes, he's sure," Sean says. "C'mon, D. Let's go." He turns his back to me and begins walking. Fast.

Denver looks at me. I nod. "Go. I'm going to stop and feed Moose, anyway."

Denver sighs and hurries after his friend.

I set down my pack. Moose whines as I dig through my supplies and snaps up the handful of dog treats I feed him. I polish off a Clif Bar as he scarfs down his food, and we are off again.

The trail climbs steeply past the highway. I plod along slowly, but I don't stop. Step. Breath. Step. Breath. I chant this in my head as I climb past the tree line and into a boulder field.

I realize that even at my snail pace, I'm making better progress on my own than if I had tried to keep up with Sean and Denver. I probably would have pooped out within an hour and needed to rest for another hour. And then I would have felt bad. Now I am making my own pace. It doesn't feel speedy, but it feels right.

The wind picks up. I pull on my Windbreaker and cinch up the hood. The sky is sharp and blue, and I can see the mountains all around me—the summer green of the maple leaves, the dark spruce and pine dotting the upper elevations, valleys on either side of me, and a wave of mountains in the distance, stretching all the way to Canada.

I look at these mountains and feel the wind pressing into my cheeks and close my eyes. A little piece of me opens up to being outside, with a dog at my feet and food in my belly.

Moose and I fall into a rhythm. He bounds ahead for thirty feet, then circles back to make sure I'm still there. When he reaches me he wags his tail, gives me a drooly smile, then turns around and leaps forward again. Even though he has far more energy and strength than me, he never goes out of my sight. It's like he's afraid of losing me. It's probably just because he knows I'll give him food. But I don't mind.

Like bumps along a camel's back, we hike steadily over peak after peak. Franconia Ridge is made up of a bunch of L-named mountains—Liberty and Little Haystack, Lincoln, and finally, the beast of the range, Lafayette, which stands nearly a mile tall.

On top of Liberty, Moose and I happily wolf down a few energy bars. We pass a bunch of folks on the ridge, but I don't talk to them. I'm still trying to keep myself as forgettable as possible so no one gets suspicious and raises the alarm.

By the time we get to Little Haystack, I'm starting to slow down. Moose is running only twenty feet ahead of me instead of thirty. On Lincoln he has stopped running ahead completely. After we have another snack, Moose stays by my side, tiredly panting as we slog forward.

As the afternoon turns into evening, the steady stream of hikers trickles to one or two an hour, then none. By the time we reach the top of Lafayette, the sun has set. I pull my map out in the fading twilight and trace the trail to the Garfield Ridge Shelter. My heart sinks. I still have four miles to go.

It's cold on the rocky peak. A wind whips up, and Moose shivers. I look down at him. His head is drooping and his tongue is hanging out. He's tired, too.

I have to make a decision. Greenleaf Hut is only a mile away. I could go down to it instead of continuing on the trail. It's warm and safe.

But I said I would see Denver and Sean at the shelter, and that's what I'm going to do. I tell Moose to follow me, and we set off in the growing darkness.

CHAPTER 14

IT GETS COLDER and colder. Earlier, the wind had been cool and pleasant in the midday sun. Now it feels crueler, carving away at my body's heat minute by minute, making me squint so my eyes don't dry out. Without the sun, the mountains feel like they're turning against me.

This is the first time that I've been caught without shelter after sunset. Even snug in bed, I hate the dark. But now, with no protection, anything on the mountain can attack me.

After a half hour, even the dim twilight is gone. Night creeps up around me. All I have is the light of the stars— the moon hasn't risen yet. I can barely see the trail, and I constantly trip over rocks jutting up from the path that would have been easy to see in daylight.

Coyotes howl in the distance. It sounds like there are dozens of them. I start to panic, thinking about how easy it would be for them to surround me, rip open my pack and eat all my food, then gnaw on my arms for dessert. My breath becomes noisy shallow gulps. Every whoosh of wind, every falling rock that clatters down the mountain makes my heart jump. I swear I can see zombies moving down below.

But then Moose whines, and I know that I can't freak out. I put a hand on his trembling head. "I'm right here, buddy," I tell him. I will my voice to be steady. Both of us can't be scared. One of us has to be brave.

"Zombies can't climb this high," I whisper to myself as I descend below the tree line. The trees block out the wind, but they also make it impossible to see more than a couple of feet ahead. The thick dark presses on me from all sides as I trudge along.

I start telling Moose stories to keep my mind from going crazy with fear. "Once upon a time there was a zombie. He saw a nice juicy boy and his dog walking along a mountain and climbed up to eat them. But then a pack of coyotes surrounded the zombie and ate it instead. And the boy and the dog were safe."

Moose whimpers. I keep on talking, trying to keep both of us from being paralyzed with fright. When I run out of stories, I make up songs. "The dark is stupid; the dark is stuuuuuupid," I warble. My voice sounds small and tinny.

Moose starts to howl. "My singing isn't that bad," I tell him, but he doesn't stop. I peer into the darkness. I can't see a thing now. It's too dangerous to keep going.

I'm doomed.

Toe, your headlamp. It's Lucas's voice. In my head, saving my butt once again. Duh. I had forgotten that one of my most important pieces of equipment is sitting in the top pocket of my pack, just waiting to be used. Fear has turned my mind to mush.

Moose is still howling as I dig out my headlamp and pull the strap around my head. Even if I'm bone-tired, as long as I can see my way forward I can make it to the Garfield Ridge Shelter.

Moose is barking now. "Stop making so much noise!" I snap. "I'll get you more treats when we get to the shelter." I switch on my light and in the glare of the sudden beam I catch two dark wide-set eyes coming straight at me.

"AAAAAAAHHHH!!!" It hits me all at once—the sharp, musty smell; the coarse-haired, lumbering body; the flash of wet teeth; claws scraping the dirt. I scream again as the bear rises onto its hind legs. It towers over me and Moose, and for a second I think we are both goners.

And then the bear tips onto its back and paws at its eyes. It snorts and shakes its head, then rolls back onto its feet and crashes into the bushes, sniffling and snuffing the entire way.

I've scared a bear. My terror drains away, and I start laughing as waves of relief wash over me.

"I'm sorry," I tell Moose. "I swear I will pay more attention to you next time." In the light of my headlamp, I feed him half the Milk-Bone treats right then and there on the trail.

It is close to midnight by the time we reach the shelter. No one is inside—Sean and Denver must have set up their tent elsewhere. I'm too tired to pitch my own tent, so I lay my sleeping pad onto the wooden floor and curl up in my sleeping bag.

Moose pads wearily into the shelter. He circles a few times before collapsing next to me. He lays his head gently on my chest. I reach out and put my arm across his skinny side. He smells like rotten eggs, but I don't care.

As I drift off, I make a promise to myself to never again get caught on the trail after dark. If that bear had decided to attack me and Moose, we would have been toast. I would have never finished the trail and kept my vow to Lucas.

And even if it had just been Moose that had gotten hurt, I wouldn't have known what to do. I don't know the first thing about treating big injuries on myself, much less a dog. I probably wouldn't have been able to save him.

I can't be that irresponsible. I have to protect Moose, and that means being smarter than I was today. I should have swallowed my pride and stayed at the hut instead of charging ahead into the dark. But I wanted to prove to Sean that I could keep up with him, and it had almost ended in disaster.

Moose begins to snore. I smile and give his stinky head one last rub. "Good night, buddy," I whisper.

That night I have a dream about Lucas. We are standing at the bottom of a waterfall, but there's no water coming down.

Suddenly rivers of clear marbles ribboned with blue cascade off the top of the falls, twinkling bright globes that crack into tiny pieces as they hit the rocks next to us. I feel a wave of grief hit me at all these broken pieces, but when I look at Lucas, he is laughing.

As the shattered marbles pile up, they turn into a river of glittering light, and I realize that even broken things can turn into something beautiful.

When I wake up, for the first time in a long while, I am smiling.

CHAPTER 15

LATE-MORNING LIGHT is pouring into the shelter by the time I open my eyes. Everything aches. Even my hair hurts. I shuffle out of my sleeping bag and walk around, looking for Sean and Denver, but they aren't there. It's probably for the best. They're too fast for me, plus Sean kind of hates me. I shouldn't be following them, anyway.

But I feel a little sad at the thought of not seeing those two guys again. They saved me from the storm, maybe even saved my life. I realize I never really thanked them for doing that. Even though the chance of our paths crossing is pretty slim, I hope we get to meet one more time so I can tell them how much they helped me.

I return to the shelter and feed Moose a couple of Clif Bars that don't have chocolate in them, then chow down on two Snickers bars as I look over my map. I need to hike at least ten miles a day if I'm going to finish the trail before school starts. But I want to finish sooner. I'm starting to miss Gran. It's been a while since there's been a dog in her house, but she loves them. I can't wait for her to meet Moose.

I tap my finger on my goal for the day—Ethan Pond Shelter, a little over fifteen miles away. It's ambitious, especially considering the long night Moose and I had gone through, but I think we can do it. And if it starts getting dark, the terrain looks flat enough in the last couple of miles that I could pitch a tent anywhere along the trail.

After tucking away my map and stuffing my sleeping pad and bag into my backpack, I call to Moose. He comes trotting out of the bushes, ready to go.

First there's a steep hike that goes down past Galehead Hut. I avoid going into the hut and keep on trekking, passing a family of four slowly making their way up in the opposite direction, and letting a fast-paced group of college-age kids go by me. Beyond the hut, the trail goes straight up. Moose matches me step for step until we come to a smooth granite slab, steep-angled and slick with water. I think it's no problem until I'm halfway up it and my foot slips. My shin bangs into the rock, and I slide to the bottom of the slab. I try again, being more careful this time. Even using both my hands and feet, I can barely make it up. Moose noses to the right, then to the left of the trail, trying to find an alternate path, but short, thick spruce trees block his way. He whines uneasily.

I drop my pack and scramble down to the base of the slab. I call to Moose. He stiffens when I wrap my arms around his torso, and I wonder if he will let me pick him up. But he does not try to wriggle away. I lift him so he can reach a tiny ledge in the rock about four feet high.

My heart jumps as Moose scrabbles and slips on the nearly vertical rock, but finally his nails hitch on to the rock, and he hauls himself clear. I scramble next to him and pull on my pack, breathing a sigh of relief. We made it. Andy's lucky marble must be working.

We break above the tree line and summit South Twin and Guyot. Clouds and mist have engulfed the mountains, but as I reach the top of Guyot, the sun parts the clouds like a veil and clears the whole of the White Mountains and beyond. I turn in every direction—north, where I swear I can see Canada; south, toward the Adirondacks of New York; west, to the Franconia Ridge, from where I had come; and east, to Maine.

I'm already feeling stronger. Happier. Like I'm breaking free of my rotten luck back home. "Hey, Lucas," I whisper. "I wish you were here."

A gust of wind wraps around my words and blows them out across the mountains. Moose licks my hand, and in that moment, I am convinced that Lucas is here, grinning at the view with me.

Moose and I descend into the trees, and a few miles later we are hopping across small stream crossings. I know the next hut, Zealand Falls, is near when I hear a steady mechanical whirring and see a red-painted well pump handle moving up and down all by itself next to a large drum of a water tank.

The trail spills out next to the hut, which has a stunning view of the valley. There are two weathered front porches, divided by the front of the hut's dining room, which sticks out in between them. Each porch has a door that leads to the dining room.

I plan on passing by, but as I walk along the trail past the front decks, I hear a loud shout.

I tell Moose to stay, and jog up the steps to one of the hut porches. As I approach the door, I hesitate. Angry words are bulleting out of the hut like rapid machine-gun fire.

My heart jitters into my throat. I don't want to walk into an argument or a fight. I'm about to turn around and hurry past the hut when six words come sailing out the kitchen, hitting me straight in both ears.

"What am I going to dooooo?"

It is a cry of despair. I need to at least know what is going on. I peer in through the small rectangles of glass on the door but can't see anything.

I lean over and peek through the front window of the hut. Past the empty dining hall I can see a guy standing in the kitchen, hopping up and down in the middle of a spreading puddle of hacked-up vegetables and soup water. A fallen cooking pot lies sideways under the sinks next to a broken wooden spoon.

As the soup water runs down the wooden floorboards into the dining room, he makes a beeline for a mop in the corner of the kitchen. He picks up the mop just as his foot slips. He goes sailing backward, and his head hits the floor with a thud. "Ow," he moans.

He needs help. I swallow my shyness and barge into the hut. I drop my pack on a dining room bench and run into the kitchen. It appears as though the cook has given up on the whole situation. He tries to sit up, winces, and decides to lie back on the floor. His Carhartts and red plaid shirt and dirty-blond hair drink up the soup water.

I walk over to his head and peer down. "Hi," I say.

"Mmf," he says.

"Do you need help?"

"Nah, I'm good. Just gonna hang out down here and look at the ceiling and count some spiderwebs." The guy darts his eyes to the corners of the room, but he doesn't move his head. "Do you see four? I see four."

I look up. "Yeah, I see four."

"Good." The guy rolls slowly onto his side and gingerly pulls himself up to sitting. "Means I don't have double vision."

I pick up the fallen mop. "Hey, why don't you stay there for a second. I'll take care of this." The guy doesn't protest, and I wipe up the soup water, wringing out the mop in a drainage tub underneath a line of dish sinks. The guy goes up a narrow flight of stairs behind the kitchen to change out of his wet clothes while I find a broom and dustpan and sweep up the celery and onions, dumping them in a compost bucket on top of the sink. By the time he comes back down, in a fresh blue T-shirt and jeans, there is barely any evidence that a disaster had taken place.

The guy sticks out his hand. "Hi. I'm Jake. Thanks for helping out."

"Tony." I shake Jake's hand. "How's your head?"

"Not so great, but I don't think I have a concussion. I need to get cracking, though. I'm already behind on my cook day."

"Would you like some help?" I know I should get going, but part of me wants to stay here a while longer. Hiking until midnight the night before is beginning to catch up with me. I can feel exhaustion tugging at my legs and eyelids. Right now, cooking for an hour sounds a lot better than getting back on the trail. Plus, there aren't any guests in the hut. I don't feel like I could get found out at any moment. I straighten up and try to look more chef-like. "I've been helping my grandma in the kitchen since I was nine."

Jake furrows his eyebrows. It looks like he's about to say no, but then he sighs and hands me a cutting board and a knife. "That would be awesome, actually. I would ask another crew member to help, but they all just left for some long day-hikes, and I don't think any of them are going to be back until dinner. Can you dice onions and celery and carrots?"

CHAPTER 16

I SET UP the cutting board on one of the kitchen counters and get to work while Jake hauls out frozen balls of ham to defrost, then sets a soup pot on one of the stove burners and pours a quart of olive oil into it from a two-gallon jug. He switches on the propane flame, and I dump chopped vegetables into the soup pot when my cutting board fills up. Soon the air is filled with the sounds and smells of hissing, cooking onions. Jake adds some frozen minced garlic, then fills the pot with water, pours in a few gallons of beans, and sets the stove flame low. Before he puts a lid on, he drops a handful of metal spoons into the pot.

"Keeps the soup from burning," he tells me. "Now we let that simmer until dinner. Meanwhile, want to make some oatmeal honey bread?" Jake digs into the fridge and pulls out a three-pound bag of industrial yeast held closed with a bright green plastic clothespin. He asks me to measure out a half cup of yeast into a large bowl, and then adds a generous dose of honey, a handful of salt, and some carefully measured warm water.

I watch the yeast form little bubbles as it gobbles up the sugar in the honey. My mouth starts to water as the soup's delicate smells waft through the kitchen. All of a sudden a wave of homesickness hits me. I want to be back in Gran's kitchen, smelling soup on the stove.

"Hey. You okay?" Jake is looking at me curiously.

I nod. "Yeah. Sorry. I was just thinking about how my grandma would have loved this kitchen."

Jake smiles and pulls out two twenty-gallon rolling bins from underneath a stainless-steel island. One bin contains oatmeal; the other is full of flour. He measures out sixteen cups of flour while I measure out ten cups of oatmeal, and we dump them into the bowl. Jake kneads the dough just until it holds together, then flours the island and upturns the dough onto it. He splits the dough in two pieces and nudges one of them over to me. "And now comes my favorite part of baking," he announces. "Kneading."

Jake shows me how to work the dough, sliding his fingers under the bottom of it and lifting and folding it in half, then using the heels of his hands to push the dough back into itself. I can see why he likes it. There is something soothing to the rhythm of kneading, and how a sticky mess of unformed dough, with time and care and patience and work, transforms into a silky round ball.

Once the dough is smooth and elastic, we transfer it back to the bowl and let it rise while we make dessert. Jake decides on chocolate brownies with mint icing. He melts chocolate and butter while I beat together confectioners' sugar and milk with a dash of peppermint extract. Before long, the brownies are in the oven and we have gone back to the oatmeal honey dough, dividing it into six pieces and tucking them into oiled bread pans.

We let the bread rise a second time while we pull the brownies out of the oven. Once they're cool, we drizzle the icing over them. After a round of dishes, the bread goes in the oven, the kitchen is shipshape, and Jake and I are ready for a sit-down. Before our break, I go outside to see how Moose is doing. He is fast asleep under the porch. He's earned a nap. I give him a gentle pat and tiptoe back inside.

Jake leaves out a little bell at the front desk for guests to ding if they need him, and we head upstairs to the crew quarters.

At the top of the steps we reach a dark, tiny landing and duck through a hobbit-sized doorway. Crew rooms are off-limits to guests, and I feel like a VIP as I enter a sunlit room filled with traces of the current crew and crews past. Handwritten notes, photos of people doing handstands on hut roofs at sunset, drawings of elephants on skates and clowns riding unicorns, a poster of Han Solo marked up with pink hearts that float around his face, plus a number of battered road signs only hint at countless stories that the crew have been part of and created over the years.

Jake picks up a Calvin and Hobbes comic book and settles down on the top of a bunk bed, one of five beds in the room. There is a hammock rigged up in the center of the room, and I sink into it.

Lucas would have loved this. He would have been asking a million questions, starting with the pink hearts around Han Solo. I start to ask Jake about the *Star Wars* poster when something else catches my eye.

"What's that?" I ask, pointing to a cup of spoons. It is perched below a window that opens up into the dining room and has a few coils of fishing line wrapped around the cup handle.

Jake looks up from his comic book. "Oh, that? It's a booby trap. Have you ever heard of a night raid?"

I shake my head.

"Night-raiding is a time-honored tradition of sneaking into another hut in the dead of dark and stealing as many special objects as we can without getting caught. If you take a look at the hut dining rooms, you'll see objects that the crews have collected over the years and hung up for decoration. Road signs, mostly. Some of the objects are more coveted than others and are often booby-trapped to make them more difficult to steal."

"Like what?"

"Well, back in the 1950s and 1960s the prize item was a human skull that had been smuggled out of an abandoned logging camp. In 1969, a Cessna plane crashed on Mount Washington and its front propeller made it into the huts, though it disappeared a few years back."

Jake scratches his chin. "There's a stuffed pink boa constrictor named Vicky. A megaphone taken from Rutgers

University." He nods at the cup. "Take a peek at where that fishing line goes and tell me what you see."

I hop out of the hammock to inspect the cup. The fishing line is almost invisible, but I trace it out the window and down to the handle of a weathered rowing oar hanging on the dining room wall. "An oar?"

"Yep. That oar is one of the special items. It was used in the Olympic Games in the 1970s. Right now it's the most valuable raid item in the huts. If someone tries to take it down, they'll trigger the fishing line to tip over the cup, spilling the spoons and waking us up. There is also a row of spoons hidden behind the oar, so even if the fishing line is cut, there would still be a ruckus if the oar is moved." Jake grins. "Every once in a while a guest gets hit with a falling spoon, but they're generally good-natured about it when we explain its purpose."

Jake returns to his comic book, and I go back to the hammock. I pull a blanket over myself and fall asleep to the smells of baking bread and cooling brownies.

CHAPTER 17

"POWER RAAAAAAIIIIID!!!"

I awaken to the sound of spoons clattering and voices shouting in the dining room. Jake is halfway out the door and pounding down the stairs before I tumble out of the hammock. The cup is no longer there. I rush to the window—it has been yanked down and lies broken amid the tossed spoons on the dining room floor.

A girl with brown hair pulled into a tight ponytail is holding the paddle of the oar while a guy with spiky blue hair and a tie-dyed T-shirt is using a Swiss Army knife to slice the fishing line off the handle. Another guy, with dreadlocks, has climbed on top of one of the benches and is busily removing a No Parking sign from the wall.

My heart jumps into my throat. I want to run down there and tackle the raiding crew, but the guys pulling down the oar look big. And determined. I feel helpless. I'd be easy for them to squash like a bug if I tried to fight them.

Jake comes into view, a howling tornado of protest. He grabs the middle of the oar and leaps onto a dining room table, wrapping his body into a human knot around the wooden shaft. "You're not getting the oar, Pete," he yells.

"Hi, Jake!" the blue-haired guy says cheerfully. "I do believe I *am* getting the oar. Hannah, check and see if anyone's upstairs. We need to make sure that Jake's the only one around."

The girl with the ponytail nods. Panicked, I duck down from the window and crawl under the bunk bed as I hear footsteps climb the stairs. I scrunch up and try to make myself as still and silent as possible.

Two neon-yellow sneakers appear in the doorway. I can see flecks of mud and dirt on the shoelaces as they wind up to make little bows below a pair of gray wool socks. The sneakers step into the room and approach the bunk bed. They are so close. I swear the girl can feel my heart thumping like a jackrabbit's against the wooden floor.

"Pete, there's no one up here!" Hannah calls down from the window.

The neon sneakers take one more turn around the room before they finally leave, and I remember to breathe again. I wriggle out from under the bed and take a quick look through the crew window.

"George, get the duct tape!" Pete barks to the dreadlocked guy, who is trying unsuccessfully to peel Jake off the oar. George grabs a roll of tape and tosses it to Hannah before joining Pete.

Together the two burly guys pry Jake off the oar—first his fingers, then his arms, then his legs and reluctant feet.

Hannah is waiting with duct tape. They hold him down while she winds the tape around his hands and his ankles until he is completely immobile. With a flourish, Pete rips off one last piece of tape and seals it across Jake's mouth.

Once Jake is taped up, Pete, Hannah, and George go to town on the dining room, unscrewing bolts and pulling out nails to free all the decorations until the walls are bare. They pile up the signs they have taken and tie them to wooden packboards they have brought with them before carrying them to the front porch.

Pete picks up the oar and lashes it to his packboard using a length of twine. He takes his time, looping and knotting the twine tightly to make it extra secure. He gives the oar a loud kiss and carries it reverentially to the porch. When he returns, he smacks his lips together. "Snack time, anyone?"

Pete and the other two raiding crew members disappear below me, into the kitchen. I hear them shuffling about, raiding more than just signs and the oar.

Jake has been placed on top of a dining room table. He looks up and sees me. His head tilts a little and his eyes fixate on the front porch for a moment, then jump back over to me.

I know what he wants me to do. It scares me. I can handle the woods. I don't know if I can handle people. Especially confident, ridiculously in-shape college kids who would kill me if they caught me.

C'mon, Toe. Don't be a chicken. It's Lucas. In my head again.

I take a deep breath and look around the crew room. On the table next to the radio, a pair of pink scissors is jammed into a widemouthed mason jar along with black permanent markers and pens. I pick up the scissors. My hands are shaking so hard that I nearly jab myself as I tuck them in my pocket.

There is a door in the crew room that leads to a metal catwalk over the backyard. I open it quietly and tiptoe across it. The kitchen windows are open and directly below me. I can hear Pete laughing as he crunches on something. I reach the end of the catwalk and make a wide counterclockwise circle to the front of the hut.

Ducking below the dining room windows, I drop to my hands and knees to crawl over to the packboards on one of the porches. Both porch doors have been propped wide open, and I can see Jake slumped on the front dining room table. He slides his eyes over to me, and I give him a quick nod.

As quietly as I can, I begin cutting the twine pinning the oar to Pete's packboard. My hands wobble like crazy. Pete tied some good knots, and it takes several tries before they give way to the multipurpose shears.

"Yo, Jake, want some crackers?" The voice sounds like it's right next to me.

I look up. George is standing in front of Jake holding a box of Triscuits. He only has to swing his head left to see me through the doorway, a twelve-year-old nothing of a kid, crouched above the most precious raid item in the entire huts system.

George rips off the duct tape keeping Jake silent. He pulls out a cracker and makes dive-bombing sounds as he swoops it toward Jake's mouth. The cracker starts curving left.

"Hey, man, can you stir the soup and take out the bread?" Jake asks.

"Yeah, no problem." The cracker flies back to center and is fed to Jake. George throws a handful of Triscuits down the hatch, then heads back to the kitchen, munching.

I slide my hands around the center of the oar and hoist it up. The paddle end is heavier than I realize, and it rises two inches before gravity takes over and it thunks gently onto the floorboards.

I wince. One of the raid crew must have heard me. I wait a few agonizing seconds, but no one comes out to inspect the noise. I breathe in quiet shallow gulps as I shift my grip and swing the oar sideways. Waddling under the weight, I move off the porch.

There is a short bark. Moose runs over to me, his tail wagging. He has woken from his nap at exactly the wrong moment.

"Shh." I bend down to quiet him, nearly ramming the oar into the ground. I swing it up at the last second and motion for Moose to follow me down the trail. When we get about twenty yards away from the hut I hear someone shouting. We've been found out.

I crash off the trail and into the woods. I nearly eat dirt when the oar dips down and rams into the ground. I sprawl forward and just barely catch myself on Moose's skinny back. He whines and holds still while I get my feet back under me.

I yank the oar level again and keep going, trying to keep all eight feet of it from wobbling out of balance again. It seems to bang on every bush and tree that I pass, but it doesn't hit the ground again.

A hundred yards later, I stop, panting hard. I prop the oar against a maple tree and quiet my breath. I wait for the sounds of pursuit, but none come. I sit on a rock with Moose by my side and we wait.

After an hour, I am convinced that I've waited long enough. I carry the oar back until I can see the trail, then stash it behind an old rotting log.

When I get back to the hut, the signs on the front porch are gone. I tell Moose to stay outside and head in. Jake is in the kitchen, digging a spoon into a pint of Ben & Jerry's Chunky Monkey ice cream. When he sees me, he grins. "You got the oar?"

I nod.

Jake laughs. "The crew from Greenleaf are mighty mad. They couldn't figure out where it went. I think I've convinced them that Zealand has a ghost thief."

Ghost thief. I could get used to the name. Sounds wily.

Jake goes to the freezer and removes a second pint. It's Phish Food. Chocolate ice cream with chocolate fish swimming in marshmallows swirls. My favorite.

Jake hands me the pint and a spoon. "For you."

"Where'd you get it?"

"Whether or not a raid is successful, it is tradition for raiding crew members to offer tokens of consolation to the crew that gets raided. In this case, we are the lucky winners of two pints of Ben and Jerry's."

"So that was a power raid," I say as Jake and I gobble and slurp down our pints.

"Yup," Jake says, licking his spoon. "It's more risky than a night raid. If any of my crew had stayed around, we could have shut them down." He pats me on the back. "But they weren't. And we still have the oar. I'm glad you were here, Tony."

After we finish the ice cream, I show Jake where I hid the oar, and we spend the afternoon rigging it to the wall. When we are done, it is the only decoration in the dining room. But it is enough. As I stare at one of the silver spoons peeking out from the oar's paddle, a flicker of pride shoots through me. I did it. I helped Jake out and didn't screw everything up. I can protect things.

It feels like my bad luck is turning. I think of Andy's marble, safely tucked away in my pack. Once again, it seems to be working.

CHAPTER 18

AS EVENING COMES, Jake invites me to grab a spare bunk and spend the night. I look around the hut. It is nearly six o'clock, and most of the guests spending the night have already arrived. There are at least two dozen people milling around the dining room. It's too dangerous. Too many people.

Then again, my goal for the day, Ethan Pond Shelter, is still five miles away. I don't want to be stuck making camp after dark again. I've already learned that lesson. "Do you know any place nearby where I could camp?" I ask Jake.

Jake nods. "There's a stealth site just down the trail. Once you come to an intersection and take a right, start looking on your right. You'll see it in a few hundred feet."

"Thanks. I think I'll set up there for the night," I tell him. "Too many people snore in the bunk rooms." I don't want to tell him the real reason I've been avoiding the huts at night.

Before I leave, Jake gives me an extra loaf of bread for the road. "Be careful," he warns me. "It's gonna be a scorcher of a day tomorrow."

Moose is waiting for me on the steps outside of the hut. I tear off a few hunks of bread and toss them to him. "C'mon, boy," I say. "Let's get going."

We head down a short, steep rocky section that ends abruptly in smooth, flat ground. I take a right at the intersection and start hunting for the stealth site like Jake told me to. Even though he told me it was easy to find, it takes a few back-and-forths before I spot the narrow bushwhack trail leading down to it.

I set down my pack and fire up my stove, cooking up two boxes of Annie's mac and cheese. As I spoon out half on the ground for Moose to eat, it occurs to me that I should be getting him some proper dog food. And a dog bowl. And maybe a leash for when we have to cross real roads. To keep him safe.

It'll add a couple of pounds to my pack. And it'll cost more than I budgeted for. I think about the shrinking roll of bills in my backpack. I would have to be very careful to have enough to buy food for me plus Moose.

I look over at Moose, where he is lapping up his dinner in fast, hungry gulps. He looks up with his scruffy face and gives me a huge doggy smile, and I know he's worth it.

As soon as he has gobbled up every bite of his dinner, Moose trots over to where I'm sitting with my pot of macaroni. He noses his way in between my legs. I lift up my pot and look down at him. He woofs and wags his tail. I shake my head. "No, you can't have my dinner," I scold him.

Moose raises his eyebrows and gives me the most pathetic sad little puppy eyes look. It completely destroys me. "Oh, you are good," I grumble. I reach into my pack and pull out the rest of the bread. I decide to eat fast, so by the time Moose is done with his dinner, my plate is empty and I'm not tempted to give him more macaroni.

As I gobble down the rest of my dinner, I pull out my map. It's thirteen miles to Mizpah Spring Hut, the next hut down the trail. There's a tentsite nearby, where I figure I can stay for my next night.

Thirteen miles. I smile to myself. When I first started out, I was barely making ten miles a day. I thought it would be a miracle if I could hold the pace. Now, after nearly a week on the trail, and especially after the mileage I pulled yesterday, I know I can make it.

I lick the last bit of mac and cheese off my spoon and stand up. There is a small stream nearby, and I walk down to it to clean my cookware. As I'm finishing up, I hear barking from the campsite.

Moose. He's in danger.

I grab my stuff and run back to the site in time to see Moose circling a great big bearded man wearing a dirty rust-colored backpack.

I'm about to scream at the man, to tell him to get away from my dog, when the man stoops down to Moose and holds his hand out.

"Here, boy," he says. His voice is deep and calm.

My stomach flips back right side up as I see him reach over and gently scratch behind Moose's ears. "Hi," I say hesitantly.

The man looks up. "This your puppy?"

I nod. "Moose, settle."

Moose trots over to me. I reach down and scratch his belly. "Be good."

The man straightens. "Mind if I camp here with you tonight? I'm thru-hiking and didn't want to stay at the hut, so they told me to come this way."

"Not at all." A jolt of excitement jumps through me. I've never met a bona fide thru-hiker before. "I'm Toby." My real name slips out before I can catch it.

The man nods. "Name's Wingin' It."

"Wingin' It?"

"It's my trail name. When I'm in town I like to order buckets of chicken wings and chow down." He shrugs. "I also don't plan much." He sets down his pack. "Hate to be rude, but I gotta get something to eat before my gut digests itself."

Wingin' It gets to work on his dinner while I pitch my tent, driving the stakes into the rocky ground. After I set down my sleeping pad and fluff up my bag, I jam all my food into my bear bag and go to find a place to sling it up. As I walk by Wingin' It, he is just settling into his dinner, a massive helping of ramen noodles. I spot four empty noodle packages curled up in a plastic trash bag.

Wingin' It is on the ground leaning back against a fallen log. "Sit down and have a chat," he tells me.

If I had been Lucas, I would have already been bugging Wingin' It with a million questions. What's the whole trail like? What was your favorite part? Did you ever almost give up, and if so, where and why?

But I'm not Lucas. I'm me. The kid standing behind the kid asking the questions.

I hesitate. I'm about to tell Wingin' It that I'm just going to hang up my bear bag and go to bed, but then Moose trots over to the thru-hiker and casually plops down next to him. He gives Wingin' It his devastating puppy eyes look.

Wingin' It picks out one long string of ramen and dangles it in front of Moose. Moose catches it on his nose and licks it up.

I sigh. If Moose is going to be social, then so am I. I settle against the fallen log and stare as Wingin' It wolfs down the steaming noodles. He eats faster than Moose. When he's finished with the ramen, he slurps down the soup and belches. "That was good." He sighs. "When you're hiking miles upon miles every day, there's just no way that you can keep up with feeding yourself. You're ravenous all the time."

"What's the hungriest you have felt?" I ask.

Wingin' It gives me a long, contemplative stare. "Now that's a story," he says slowly. "I'll tell you for some dessert."

I dig through my bear bag and pull out two Snickers bars. Wingin' It solemnly accepts them. He peels open the wrapper on one of them, bites down, and chews appreciatively. When he has licked the chocolate off his fingers, he is ready to begin.

CHAPTER 19

"SOME WEEKS AGO I was on this one stretch down in Vermont. It's a piece of trail where you'll cross a couple of country roads, but you won't see a single gas station or convenience store the whole way. It's about three days of travel before you can even think about a resupply.

"I was traveling with another thru-hiker, named Arsenic. I had met him in Connecticut, shortly after passing the New York state line. We hiked at the same pace, so we more or less found ourselves camping together for about two weeks before we got to those three days in Vermont.

"I didn't particularly like Arsenic—he was always bumming cigarettes and food off other hikers, even though he had more than enough of his own supplies. And he wasn't exactly a bluebird in springtime when it came to personality. He was rough. He had been in the army. It had . . . done things to his head. Served three tours in Afghanistan, came home angry and broken and decided to hike the trail.

"While I hiked with Arsenic, I had to listen to hour-long rants about the messed-up things that humans can do to one another. At first, the stories that Arsenic told made me more than a little afraid of him—this was a guy whose job description included shooting people, after all. But as the days went by, I realized that Arsenic didn't enjoy watching or participating in the dark side of human nature. He was mad that he had to be part of it.

"That first day in Vermont, Arsenic and I had booked it pretty hard and got twenty-three miles from the last town before we set up camp for the night. We were stopped at a shelter, just the two of us. It was pretty late for trail time, about seven o'clock, with the sun hurrying down toward the horizon.

"We left our dinners inside the shelter—three packets of ramen noodles each—and went out to hang the rest of our food.

"We were rigging our bear bag and had been able to throw our rope over a high branch of a beech tree. We had tied the sack with all our food to the rope and I was just starting to haul it up when we saw this shape coming out from the shadows. It was covered with shaggy black fur, and it was very, very big."

"A bear," I breathe. Not a funny one, like the one Moose and I had run into last night.

Wingin' It nods. "Not just a bear. A hungry bear." Wingin' It reaches for a water bottle and takes a deep swig. "Coming face-to-face with something with claws and teeth—something that will eat meat, and realizing that in the end, you are potentially just another meal for a wild animal—is a frightening thing.

"And here we are, with all our food on an open sack on the ground and a massive black bear lumbering our way. Arsenic goes running, and I am left holding the rope. In that moment I have to make a decision. Run for it, and lose whatever food the bear decides to eat, or try and scare it away."

"What did you do?" I ask. I know what I would have done. Run like heck.

Wingin' It blinks slowly, remembering. "I let go of the rope and hoofed it back to the shelter. Arsenic was there, too. We watched in dead silence as that bear tore into the dry sack and had himself a fine old dinner at our expense. He ate every last bit of our food, snuffling around to pick up the crumbs he might have left behind. When he was done, he gave this satisfied grunt and waddled back into the shadows of the woods.

"And when Arsenic and I finally turned away from the scene of carnage to our ramen noodles behind us, we discovered that some manner of chipmunks or mice had gotten to it. They had chewed through the plastic ramen packages, leaving only sad curls of broken noodles scattered across the wooden floor."

"That night Arsenic and I swept the fragments of noodles into one cooking pot and had ourselves a miserable dinner that tasted like half food, half boot dirt. We had to decide if we were going to backtrack for a resupply, adding almost twenty-five extra miles to our journey, or if we were going to press on and hope that we would find people with extra food that they could give us.

Even though I've had dinner, my stomach growls at the thought of hiking for so long with so little food. "What did you do?" I asked again.

"Arsenic and I made different decisions. Arsenic was convinced that even if we ran into people, they wouldn't spare us any food. He decided to backtrack. In all honesty, his pessimism was practical. But I had faith that I would be able to get by."

Wingin' It takes another sip of water. "The next morning we said good-bye to each other and parted ways. By mid-afternoon I was starting to think that Arsenic had been right, and by nightfall I was convinced of it. I had crossed a road and waited four hours for a hitch to a town. A couple of cars passed, but no one picked me up, so I kept going. I didn't see a single human soul over the nineteen miles I traveled that day. The only food I had had was a few chocolate smears that had been left inside a Hershey's bar wrapper that I found at around mile twelve.

"That night there was a cold snap, and I found myself shivering like a wet dog inside my sleeping bag. I didn't have enough calories to keep warm. When dawn came, I was shaking so hard from hunger that I could barely stand up.

"I made it about twelve more miles, and then I was done. I staggered and fell, and no amount of willpower was going to get me back up again. And so I dragged myself to a tree by the side of the trail and sat. And waited.

"I was there for six hours. Just waiting, too tired to swat the mosquitoes slurping away at my blood and the flies buzzing about my ears. And as evening crept on and the sun began to set, I heard someone coming down the trail. I cleared my throat and begin to call out for help. And who should answer but a familiar, irritated voice. It was Arsenic.

"He had backtracked, filled his pack with food, and then hitchhiked to a spot on the highway, bushwhacked to the shelter where we had met the bear, and had started hiking to find me. When he did, he cursed and muttered and called me all sorts of things that amounted to the fact that I was an idiot, all the while putting pieces of chocolate into my mouth as if I were a baby sparrow.

"An hour later, I was able to get up and help pitch a tent, and a week later, it was me who Arsenic leaned on for over six miles, as he hopped out of the wilderness on a broken ankle."

A quiet descends. Wingin' It tips back his water bottle and finishes the last of his water. He turns to me. "Thanks for the dessert," he says.

"Thanks for the story," I tell him. I get to my feet. It's full dark now, and tomorrow both of us have big days ahead of us. I say good night to Wingin' It and find a tree to hang my bear bag.

That night I dream that a pack of hungry bears are chasing me with their open claws and mouths. When I wake the next morning, Wingin' It has already packed up and left, and it's just me and Moose again.

CHAPTER 20

JAKE WAS RIGHT. Unlike the numbingly cold rainstorm that nearly ended my hike a few days ago, today the air wraps around me like a hot, slobbery tongue. Heat rises from the ground, rippling the summer leaves. There is no wind. As I slog forward, my eyes begin to droop and my feet get sluggish.

Moose starts off racing ahead of me, but soon the heat gets to him, too, and he's matching my snail's pace. By midday we have covered seven hilly miles of trail and crossed over Route 302 to tackle the other side of the valley. Here the trail goes up sharply. I battle gravity and the heat. My world shrinks to my feet and the dirt in front of them. Step. Step. Step. Plod. Plod. Plod.

My palms are greasy with sweat. I am hot. Hotter than baked pizza. Hotter than a cactus in the sun. Hotter than Mount Vesuvius. When it's erupting.

The heat does not quit. I mop my forehead and stare out at the trail ahead me. I swear it is shimmering with heat.

I see a boulder up ahead. All of me wants to lie down on it and go to sleep.

Keep on going. We're nearly there, Toe. It's Lucas's voice inside my head. Telling me what to do again.

I check my map. I still have five miles to go before the tentsite near Mizpah Hut. Despite the heat, I shiver. Lucas is wrong.

Just like the last time he said that.

It was when we were doing number five on the List.

We had already done *#2: Eat a worm.* That was the hardest one of all, I'd thought at the time. The day after our fishing trip, I got up early, when the grass was still wet with dew, to dig up the worms from Lucas's backyard. My stomach was a pile of knots. I couldn't promise myself that I wouldn't upchuck the worm as soon as it touched my tongue.

When I arrived, Lucas was wearing a chef's apron that seemed to swallow his whole body and a white poufy hat. "We are going to have the most delicious worms in the history of worm eating!" he told me. He showed me a bucket and a spade. "You go dig up the worms. Leave the rest to me."

I went outside and dug the spade into the soft ground. When I pulled it out, there were at least six or seven worms writhing in the clod of dirt. I hurriedly dropped it into the bucket and ran back into the kitchen, my stomach churning.

Lucas took the bucket. He made a big show of washing the worms, then drying them carefully with a square of paper towel. Next, he melted a stick of butter in a cast-iron pan and tossed the wiggling worms inside, frying them up. He looked over at me, grinning maniacally as I tried to ignore the smell of cooking worms and the sizzle of the hot butter.

I had almost backed out when I saw the limp gray squiggles in the pan, but Lucas knew exactly how to get me to eat them. He had toasted two buns until they were golden brown, drenched them in more butter, and laid a worm in each bun. Finally, he had pulled out bottles of Heinz and French's and squirted ketchup and bright yellow mustard until I could barely see the worms. We had sat on his front steps and had eaten them like extra-skinny, extra-chewy hot dogs.

They weren't bad.

The next to go was #3: *Spend a whole day at the movie theater.* We paid for a 10:00 a.m. showing and stumbled out ten hours later, our bellies lurching with popcorn, having watched five movies on one ticket each.

For number four, Lucas's dad helped us nail together a tree house using scrap wood from an old barn that had been torn down. We spent entire afternoons in that rickety thing, playing cards and reading comics, ready to dash down the rope ladder if a creaky board gave way.

Then came number five—blueberry picking. Two weeks after building our tree house, we took two gallon metal buckets and went up a local mountain in search of blueberries.

Lucas, as always, was in the lead. His dad had shown him a supersecret blueberry picking spot the year before, and he wanted to show it to me by himself.

We climbed and climbed for hours, finally getting to the bald summit at noon. Blueberry bushes were everywhere, but a lot of them had been picked over. The mountain was known as the blueberry spot for miles around. People had even seen commercial blueberry pickers combing through the bushes with rakes.

Lucas wasn't worried, though. "C'mon, Toby. The spot I'm thinking about isn't on the path. We'll be sure to find gallons of blueberries there."

"Is it close?" I peeked up at the sky. The noonday sun was blazing overhead, and I was nearly out of water.

"So close," he told me.

He led us off the main path, bushwhacking through thigh-high bushes that scraped against my legs and made me itch. After an hour, I was ready to stop. My arms were lobster red from sunburn. I had forgotten to wear a hat. I didn't even want to think about what my face looked like. "How much longer?" I asked.

"Just a little bit farther." But now Lucas didn't sound so sure.

"Well, you'd better be right."

"Keep on going. We're nearly there."

But we weren't. We wandered until our water was gone and our skin started to peel and blister. When crows began to circle above, I swear they were waiting for us to drop so they could eat us.

Finally Lucas called it off. "We'll find it next time," he said.

"Next time? Next time?" I laughed. "Some supersecret spot you found."

"Well, you haven't been much help," Lucas snapped tiredly. "Why don't you try taking charge for once?"

"How am I supposed to lead when I don't even know where we're going?"

"Is it my fault that I'm always the one who has to know where we're going? And that you never even bother to try to help out?"

"Well, is it my fault that you never let me be first?" I shouted.

"You never want to!" Lucas shouted back.

"Sure I do." I said the words, knowing that they were a lie.

"Yeah, right." Lucas rolled his eyes. "You're just like a little lost puppy, Toby. Following me wherever I go."

Anger rose in my throat. "Well, guess what. You need me following you around to feel important. To feel like you're in charge." I was so mad I could spit. Only, I was so dehydrated I didn't have enough saliva to even do that. "Except now you've screwed up, and you don't want to admit it."

"Let's just find the trail and get back down," Lucas said stiffly.

"Fine." I was too tired and hot to argue more. I had trusted Lucas to lead. To know where to go and what to do. Instead, he had failed. For the first time, he had failed me.

We backtracked until we hit the main path, then hiked down in complete silence. When we got to my house, I turned my back to him and went up the front steps without saying good-bye.

Later that night, when I was getting ready for bed, Gran came into my room. She handed me a little glass jar. "I found this on the porch. I think it's for you."

Inside the jar was a single blueberry. A Post-it note was stuck to the lid. Lucas's handwriting, of course.

#5. ~~Go blueberry picking~~
Sorry about losing the way.

CHAPTER 21

NUMBER FIVE. NUMBER five was when things between me and Lucas started to go wrong. I began seeing ways that Lucas was not perfect. How he could mess up, just like me. He had been my good-luck charm, and he had failed me.

I hear a low growl of excitement. I look up and instantly forget about Lucas. "Moose. Moose, no."

Moose has torn into the woods, barking furiously as he scrambles past a thicket of young spruce. His prey is small and furry and slow. It ambles unhurriedly through the brush, snuffling through the dirt for grubs. It is way too easy to catch.

"*Mooooose!*" My pack is on the trail, and I go crashing through the brush. "Come back, boy!"

Moose does not listen. By the time I get to him, the skunk is already hissing and stamping, its tail puffed out so wildly it looks like it has been stuffed into an electric socket.

"Hey there, boy." I try to keep my voice even. "Moose, you leave him alone."

Moose perks up his ears. He hears me, but his eyes are fixed on the skunk. Slowly he lowers his head. A woof escapes his throat. He begins to circle the black-and-white ball of fur.

The skunk hisses again, and Moose rushes it. The skunk backs away and turns its tail toward Moose.

"Moose, stop!" I cry, but Moose is in full-on attack mode. With a snarl, he darts forward, his mouth gaping open as he goes in for the kill.

The skunk blasts him with a putrid yellow spray that lands squarely on Moose's nose. He sneezes and snuffs, and lets out a piteous moan, as if hot coals have been thrown on his snout. His hind legs collapse on him as he paws at his face. Satisfied, the skunk hurries on its unharmed way.

"Oh, Moose." I want to hug him, but the stink is overwhelming. Moose drops to the ground and rolls around, trying to escape the horrible smell covering his body, but only succeeds in dirtying up his already-mangy coat.

As I watch Moose, all I can think is that I've gone and done it. My bad luck has rubbed off on him. Of course the first thing I tried to take care of would get hit in the face with skunk spray.

"C'mon, boy. We'll get you cleaned up." I hope it's the truth.

It seems like ages before we reach Mizpah. It is late afternoon, and both of us are tired and stinky. Moose drops his head and lays down on a flat rock while I go inside.

Afternoon light pours through the high windows of the dining room. Leaning back on a chair behind the front desk is the most beautiful girl I have ever seen. She is wearing a denim dress cinched at the waist with a simple brown belt. Her long brown hair falls over her shoulders like waves on a beach. Her green eyes are fixed on the guitar she is strumming. Half-formed thoughts and murmurs spill from her lips. She is lost in the song that she is making.

I want to freeze that moment forever. A girl, her voice, sunlight falling on her hair.

She finishes and looks up. "Hi there."

"Um. Hi. Hello. Um." I am having trouble making words. "Yes. Well. You sing. That was really nice. Oh! Yes. Skunk."

I think I am babbling.

"Oh no." The angel puts down her guitar. "Pepper." She sighs. "He's been hanging around the hut for the past month. At some point he was bound to spray."

"I tried to stop him, but he got to Moose."

The girl's lovely eyebrows arch delicately. I see the question on her face.

"I mean, he got my dog. Well, he's not my dog. But he's been following me. I named him Moose. The skunk didn't get a real moose. That would be funny. Ha-ha." My efforts to sound intelligent are not improving.

The girl comes out from behind the counter. "Let's take a look and see what we can do."

CHAPTER 22

MOOSE HAS COMPANY by the flat rock. I spot a familiar ball cap and bandanna standing a respectful distance from him.

"Sean! Denver!"

"Hey there, Tony." Denver waves. "How long have you been here?"

"Just a couple of minutes."

"Are you planning to stay the night?"

"Yeah. At Nauman tentsite, next door."

Denver nods. "Us, too. Glad to see you caught up to us. Sean and I were heading to the hut to refill our water bottles when we ran into your dog."

"It doesn't seem as though he's having a very good day," says Sean.

Moose thumps his tail sadly.

The girl from heaven turns to the pile of stench curled in a miserable ball. "This guy is going to need a good scrubbing."

"Do you need help?" Denver asks eagerly.

"The more the better," says the girl. She smiles at Denver. "I'm Abbey."

"Denver."

In that moment, I wish I were five years older and handsome and rugged and not a blubbery mess whenever I talk to a pretty girl. Denver has spoken five words, and already he's gotten the girl's name and her smile. Jealously flickers in me.

On the other hand, Sean does not seem impressed with Abbey's green eyes and long, dark, silky hair. "I'm refilling my water," he says gruffly, and heads inside the hut.

"I hear tomato juice is great at getting the stench out," Denver says to Abbey.

"No, that's a myth," I interrupt. Denver has been nice to me, but I'm eager to prove to Abbey that I know a thing or two about skunks. "It just covers the smell—it doesn't get rid of it. A few years ago, me and a friend of mine were volunteering at a rescue shelter. A dog came in after being skunked, and the way we got rid of it was with hydrogen peroxide, baking soda, and dish detergent."

Abbey pulls out her phone and double-checks my facts. "Looks like Tony is right," she says.

I silently cheer.

"We've got that stuff in the hut. We can de-skunk Moose out back. Follow me," Abbey says.

I call to Moose, and he hops off his rock. He follows me and Denver as Abbey leads us down a rugged path that cuts through grass and rocks to a hidden corner of the hut. It's like a little hideaway, surrounded by trees and protected from view of foot traffic.

It's a surprise to find a secret place so close to the hut. It's even more of a surprise to find a turquoise kiddie pool dotted with pink dolphins, full of water, with a guy in a Speedo and a forest of curly hair on his chest lounging in it, reading a copy of *Harry Potter and the Deathly Hallows*. He looks up as we approach, then goes back to his book.

As we get closer, the guy's nostrils flare. He gives two short sniffs, and then he is out of the pool and hopping about, holding his nose, as water dances off his tight swimsuit. Miraculously, Harry Potter has stayed dry.

"Pool time's over, Dan." Abbey gives Moose a tentative pat. "Pepper skunked this little guy. We've got to get him soaped up."

Dan wraps a towel around his waist. "I'll heat some water," he says, and disappears through a side door into the hut.

"Wait here." Abbey follows Dan and reappears shortly with a bottle of hydrogen peroxide, a box of baking soda, liquid soap, a sand pail, and an old threadbare towel. She mixes the de-skunking ingredients in the pail and fills it with water so it bubbles up. "Here, Moose," she calls.

Moose skitters back, whining.

"Here, let me try. I'm good with dogs." Denver rolls up his pant legs and steps into the kiddie pool. "C'mon, boy," he coaxes, clapping his hands softly.

Moose hesitates, and Denver crouches down. "Here, boy. We're going to get you cleaned up." Denver reaches for Moose and hoists him into the pool.

Moose holds still as Denver lifts him up, but as soon as his paws touch the water, he explodes. His legs pummel the air, and his body twists like a seal. He head-butts Denver, and the two of them pitch backward, sending a massive wave across the pool.

Sputtering, Denver emerges from the water still holding Moose, who is yipping in terror.

"Moose. Moose. Hey." A moment later I am in the water with them, my arms hugging Moose's stinky body. Denver has let go and is busy wiping his eyes clear of water.

I ignore the horrible reek of skunked dog hair and put my chin on Moose's head. I scratch behind his ears and whisper, "It's okay, buddy. Shhh. It's okay."

Moose trembles and quiets down. I stroke his matted fur, feeling the skin drawn tight over his still-showing ribs. Even though he has feasted on bread and pasta for the past couple of days, a lifetime of starvation has kept him horribly skinny.

Keeping one hand on his head, I dip the other in the water and slowly wet Moose down. Abbey hands me the pail, and I pour the mixture over Moose's back. I work my hand through his fur, gently scrubbing one side. I pick out twigs and untangle knots and work out clumps of dirt-encrusted hair.

Moose has closed his eyes and sits perfectly still. Where before he was frightened of the bath, I think he's enjoying it now. When I have scrubbed away all the layers of dirt, I use the empty sand pail to rinse him off.

Dan arrives with a large pot of warm water, and I pour it over Moose. When I am done, he jumps out of the pool and shakes himself off. He is clean for the first time since I met him, and now I can see that the splotch of fur on his chest is pure white. I pick up the old towel that Abbey has brought and rub him down. He still has a whiff of skunk on him, but only a whiff.

As I dry his head, Moose gives my face a single lick. It's like he's telling me that it's okay. That it wasn't my bad luck that got him, but just something bad that happened. And I figured out a way to make it better.

It is then when I feel like Moose is really and truly my dog.

CHAPTER 23

ABBEY INVITES SEAN, Denver, and me to join the crew after the guests have been served dinner. After the leftovers are scraped into mustard-colored plastic salad bowls, we feast on ham and rice, slices of challah dipped in minestrone, and boiled broccoli. The guests have gone through all the homemade dessert, so Abbey breaks out Oreos and pours us glasses of milk.

I break an Oreo in two pieces. I casually flip one half into the air and pray that it lands in my mouth and impresses the socks off Abbey.

I succeed, but a little too well. The Oreo chunk bull's-eyes my throat, and a second later I am choking and swigging down milk, coughing with little explosions that send the milk spurting out of my nose. "I'm fine," I whisper hoarsely when Dan offers to give me the Heimlich.

Denver breaks an Oreo into quarters. He takes a swig of milk and tilts his head back. A piece of Oreo flies behind his back and over his shoulder, landing with a plop in his open mouth.

"Where'd you learn to do that?" asks Abbey.

Envy wriggles through my veins again. I dab milk off my nostrils.

Denver flips another quarter of Oreo into his mouth. "My older brother, Harry. He had the sharpest eye and best aim of anyone in the neighborhood. When we were in middle school, he could pitch a dime into a water glass from fifty feet away." A third quarter of Oreo lands neatly onto his tongue. "Almost made it to the big leagues last year."

Dan lifts his eyebrows. "Why almost?"

The last piece of Oreo clicks off Denver's front tooth. He tries to grab it, but his hand goes wide and the cookie tumbles to the floor. Instead of picking it up, he just stares at it blankly.

"Did something happen to him?" I ask.

"Yes." Denver's voice is short.

A thick silence fills the air.

I shouldn't press. It would be mean, and I know it. But I'm so jealous of Denver's neat little Oreo trick that's making Abbey's eyes shine that I lose my head. I press. "Was there an accident?"

No answer. Denver's shoulders hunch. He stares mutely at the fallen cookie with dimming eyes, lost in the memory of what happened.

I know that look. Of grief and numbness and disbelief at the unfairness of life.

I've gone too far. Suddenly I feel horrible. "Hey. I'm sorry. I didn't mean to pry."

As if shaking off a nightmare, Denver's eyes come back into focus. He looks at me and sighs. "No, it's all right." He takes a deep breath. "My brother was the star of the baseball team all throughout high school. His senior year of high school, they were 18–0. Three of those games had been no-hitters. Harry threw a mean curveball, but it was his fastball that pegged him for the major leagues. He had it up to ninety-one miles per hour by the time his team got to the state championships.

"A big talent scout was going to be there. Harry was certain he was going to be drafted into the major leagues. He just had to pitch one perfect game.

"Then the night before the big game, Harry and I got into a fight. It was over something stupid—what Netflix show to watch; I don't even remember." Denver bends down and picks the piece of Oreo off the floor. He turns it in his hands, as if it is a Magic 8 Ball with all the answers. "Funny how little things can change your life.

"We ended up wrestling for the remote. At one point I grabbed it and yanked. Harry tripped over the couch. His right eye landed on the corner of the coffee table. And that was the end of his baseball career."

Without dusting off any dirt, Denver puts the Oreo in his mouth and chews. "A few weeks later he ran away from home. My parents went crazy trying to find him. But he was eighteen. Legally he could disappear if he wanted to. And he did. We haven't seen or heard from him in over a year."

Except for the soft ticking of a wall clock above the sink, it is quiet in the kitchen.

Sean puts a hand on Denver's back. "C'mon, man. Let's go to bed." He keeps his hand on Denver and guides him out the front door. As they head out, the glow of the hut light silhouettes them against the wooden floors—two shadows melting together to keep each other standing.

Later, I head over to the tentsite and set up next to Sean and Denver's tent. As I crawl in and zip up the mosquito netting, Moose hops up on the platform. He turns a couple of times before settling down in front of the tent.

As I fall asleep, I think about how surprising life is. I started on this trail because I wanted to get away from the bad luck and hurt in my life. I had run into plenty of trouble at the beginning of the trail, but right now Andy's marble seems to be protecting me. But it hasn't stopped me from running into the bad luck and hurt of others.

Yet somehow, through sharing stories of the ways life can knock you down, there's friendship. Understanding. Strength.

I think about Denver. How he's such a good guy. And how that goodness became twisted into guilt over something that wasn't his fault. He'll probably feel responsible for his brother's accident for the rest of his life. Even though it was just bad luck.

I can hear Sean and Denver shifting on their sleeping pads in the tent next to mine. I'm glad they have each other. I think about the story Denver told me about how he and Sean became friends. How they protect each other. Then I think about the story Wingin' It told me, how people are thrown into bad situations that are none of their fault, and how they figure their way through it.

Maybe life isn't about luck, good or bad. Maybe it's a lot about leaning on others when things get rough. And being leaned on in return.

Outside the tent, Moose lets out a long, slow fart.

I smile. I started alone, but we're going to finish this trail together. Me and Moose and the other half of my shadow—Lucas.

"I promise," I whisper. "I will see us through all the way to Katahdin."

CHAPTER 24

THE NEXT MORNING I wake to thick fog. A cold wind presses against the tent, and I close the vestibule to get an extra bit of warmth while I dress. Unlike the hot, sticky mugginess of the day before, this day promises to be wet and chilly.

A black nose appears in the tent the second I unzip it. I have to push Moose back so he doesn't invade my sleeping bag. He's clean, but he still smells like damp dog.

Sean is on the platform stirring oatmeal into a pot of boiling water. "There's a storm coming," he says as I clamber out of my tent.

"How can you tell?" I break out two Clif Bars and a hunk of cheddar cheese. I toss one of the bars to Moose.

"I checked the weather forecast at the hut this morning. Gusts on Washington are going to be over sixty miles an hour, and the wind chill is expected to get to about twenty degrees."

"But it was so hot yesterday!" I can't believe there could be such a huge difference in temperature in less than twenty-four hours.

Sean shrugs. "Welcome to the Whites." He takes out a jar of peanut butter and adds a couple of spoonfuls to the oatmeal mixture. We eat our breakfast in silence.

"Where's Denver?" I ask as I finish off the last of my cheese and crumple empty wrappers into my food bag.

"He left early this morning. He told me to meet him on top of Washington. Wanted to do the last bit of hiking by himself."

"That's right—you two are finishing your trip today." I feel a twinge of sadness. Denver and Sean had saved me on that rain-drenched day when I had nearly given up. Without them, I would probably have quit the trail. But now they are leaving and I will really be on my own.

I lick my bowl and spoon clean, then tuck them back in my pack. After breaking down my tent, I stop by the hut quickly to say good-bye to Abbey. I call to Moose, and as we turn back down the trail, I see Sean. He has a scowl on his face.

"Hurry up," he says.

When I tell him that he doesn't have to wait for me, his scowl deepens. "Normally I'd agree. I hate waiting for you. But you're not hiking in this weather by yourself," he says curtly. He turns his back to me and starts hiking.

I grin and follow him, with Moose not far behind.

A mile later, the rain begins. We pause for a moment to shrug into our raincoats, and I ask Sean a question that I had been wondering about since that morning. "Did you know about Denver's older brother?"

"Yeah. Denver worshipped him." Sean turns his head to the side and puts a finger over a nostril. He exhales hard, and a snot rocket flies out to the side of the trail. "When Harry disappeared, Denver nearly went crazy with guilt."

"How long ago was that?"

Sean clears the second nostril. "Come to think of it, it was exactly a year to this day that Harry ran away." He goes utterly still for a moment. "I have a bad feeling about this. Maybe I shouldn't have let Denver hike by himself this morning."

"I'm sure he's fine," I say. Nevertheless, Sean hitches up his backpack and shoots down the trail as though a swarm of bees were after us. Before long we are above the tree line. The rain has increased to a pelting clatter, and we can barely see the trail ten feet in front of us. I pull my rain hood over my head and cinch it tight. Moose whimpers. "Sorry, buddy," I tell him. There will be no shelter, no trees to break the wind, until we reach the next hut over, Lakes of the Clouds.

The higher we climb, the more the temperature drops. Without the trees to protect us, the wind rises to a sideways howl. I lean against it and hope that it keeps up. With a steady wind I can adjust my body to constantly battle the pressure. If the wind stops, I'd go tumbling.

The trail becomes all rocks and boulders, slippery with lichen and rain. It is only 4.8 miles between Mizpah and Lakes of the Clouds, but it seems like an impossible distance as our pace slows to a crawl.

A jagged arc of lightning cuts through the rain and fog. It flashes across the sky like a glowing warning finger. Moose lets out a high, frightened bark.

Nobody should be above the tree line in a lightning storm. Odds are, you're the tallest object sticking out from the mountain. The weather has just turned from bad to dangerous.

If I had been here with Lucas and his dad, there would have been no question about it. We would have turned around and gone back into the trees as fast as possible.

"I think we should go back!" I shout.

Sean doesn't answer but quickens his pace. "I need to find Denver," he says. His voice is low. Urgent. His strides lengthen. His legs are long. Too long. Behind me, Moose stumbles on a slippery boulder.

"I can't keep up!" I yell. Sean is a couple of yards ahead of me and adding more distance between us fast. He doesn't stop. I can't tell if he hasn't heard me. Or if he doesn't care.

The rain turns to hail. I tuck my head and scurry along as fast as I can, making sure that Moose is still with me. The chattering hail becomes a roar of clicking ice. I feel like I've stepped under a falling frozen waterfall. I concentrate on my boots and putting one of them in front of the other. When I finally look up, Sean is gone.

CHAPTER 25

ABANDONMENT HITS ME harder than any slap of weather. I didn't want to admit it, but I was counting on Sean and Denver to keep me safe. For their knowledge and food and gear and companionship to protect me, at least for a little bit. Now both of them have disappeared.

The wind and hail are relentless. All the energy drains out of me. Once again, I am alone in a storm.

Grief comes, hard and fast as a bullet. I sit down on a rock and put my head in my hands. I miss my best friend. "I'm sorry, Lucas," I whisper. "I can't do this. Not without help. Not without you."

I think about what had happened after the blueberry-picking disaster. We had patched things up and kept going with the List. But something felt broken between us. We had built a raft and floated down the Connecticut River, only to have it tumble apart as we were trying to land it. The night on Chimney Hill hadn't been spooky at all, but I forgot to zip up the tent door and we ended up covered in hundreds of tick and mosquito bites.

But it was when we were popping wheelies in the school parking lot that it really all fell apart. Lucas had mastered the one-wheeled trick almost immediately, but hours passed and all I had to show for it were dozens of scrapes and bruises on my elbows and knees.

"Maybe we should try again tomorrow," Lucas had said.

I hopped on my bike for one last go. I pedaled as hard as I could, then jerked my handlebars up. The bike flew over my head and I went sprawling, cracking the back of my helmet against the pavement.

Lucas rushed over and bent down to pull me up.

"Don't help me," I snapped. "I'm tired of you protecting me. You never let me get up by myself. Or stand on my own two feet."

Lucas drew back as if I had punched him in the face. "Toe, that's not true."

"Sure it is." I struggled to my feet. Blood ran down my calf. "Why do you even hang out with me? I've been nothing but bad luck since the day you met me."

Lucas shook his head. "I hang out with you because we have fun together. So what if bad stuff happens to us sometimes?"

"Or maybe you like being the hero." I could feel my tailbone throbbing. "Maybe you need me to mess up so you can fix everything. Maybe that's why you keep me around. So you can feel good about yourself."

Lucas's shoulders straightened. He walked past me

and picked up his bike. "You know what? Maybe you *are* bad luck. Maybe it's time I started making new friends."

And then Lucas had ridden away from me. He had not looked back.

A chunk of hail smashes into my shoulder and brings me back to the rock where I'm sitting. I put my hands on my cheeks. Despite the wind and ice, they are warm. I realize I am crying. And then something snaps inside of me. Big, horrible sobs wrack my chest and my lungs. I tighten my hands into fists around my hair. Alone. I am alone.

I wait for Lucas's voice to come. To comfort me and tell me what to do. But instead, there is only silence.

His voice is gone.

"Toby. Toby, get up," I tell myself. I'm speaking out loud, in the rain. "You can do this without Lucas."

No. No, you can't, says the part of me that is small and cold and scared. *You can't. You can't. You can't.* I'm drowning in my doubt. I can't even get up to save myself.

A furry snout burrows between my chin and my heart, and a long, stinky tongue licks my cheek.

"Hey, Moose." I put out a hand blindly and pat his rain-drenched side. I close my eyes. "I can do this," I tell myself.

It should have been you instead of Lucas, last summer. The awful voice of doubt is relentless. *He was the stronger one. The better one.*

I fold my arms and tuck my hands under my armpits, rocking back and forth.

Screwup, the voice whispers.

I stare into the hail as it gathers around me. Something twists inside me. I'm not going to accept my bad luck anymore. "Screwing up and giving up are two different things. Life *is* messy. Like Denver and his brother's eye. Or Arsenic in the war, or my parents and their stupid divorce. But all those people keep on going. And I'm going to, too."

You're worthless, the voice hisses. *So what if you kept going. You lost your map. You ran out of food. You couldn't keep Moose from getting skunked.*

I shake my head. "But I found my way again. I'm pointed in the right direction to Katahdin. I found food. I'm keeping Moose alive and clean and fed. I'm finally learning to trust myself." I rear back and scream with all of my might. "So screw you!"

I wait for a reply, but there is none.

A chunk of hail slips past my hood and trickles down my neck. It is ice-cold. Numbness creeps into my fingers and toes.

Moose whines and nudges my face. He is shivering.

I'm not sure I can save myself. But I am going to save this scrawny mutt of a dog if it's the last thing I do. I stand up and shake pockets of hail off my backpack and my coat. It's time to start hiking.

CHAPTER 26

MY KEEPS LIST—to keep warm, hydrated, fed, and mindful of the sun—is almost completely shot. But unlike a few days ago when Sean and Denver had to rescue me, I don't panic. I start off at a half jog to warm up. Moose trots doggedly beside me. After a few minutes, I can feel some sensation coming back into my fingers and toes. I jog until I spot a cluster of boulders that make up a little overhanging cave. Shelter from the lightning and the hail.

I urge Moose inside and skooch in beside him. The two of us barely fit, but we are both covered. I open my pack and dig out all my layers, pulling them on as fast as I can. The only things I don't put on are two T-shirts. I use one to dry off Moose. The other I wrap around his neck like a little scarf. He could use the extra warmth.

Then I take out my water bottle, gulping down liquid while tearing into a Snickers bar. Moose gets two Clif Bars. We sit and munch and huddle, keeping each other warm while I keep my eye on the weather.

The hailstorm finally lets up, giving way to a swathe of thick fog. It's still not great weather, but it'll have to do. I pack up my stuff, make sure the T-shirt around Moose is tight, and together we clamber out of the little cave and back onto the trail. As we hike, I begin to see pieces of sky through the fog. It is a moody gray, but at least it doesn't feel as though the weather is out to get us anymore.

An hour later the fog clears off, and I see two familiar Osprey packs in the distance. One is hurrying toward the other. Now that the fog is gone, the trail is easy to spot. Rock cairns as big as barrels line the way, making it fairly impossible to get lost.

But the two backpacks are not on the trail. They have veered onto a lone, sharp cliff that plummets into the valley below.

Something is wrong. I begin to run. Moose follows behind, his nails clattering against the slippery rocks.

By the time I get to them, Denver has slung off his pack and is standing at the edge of the cliff. He is so close to falling that the front of his boots are hanging over nothing but air.

"Denver, don't do this. It's not your fault," Sean is pleading.

"Yes, it is," cries Denver. "Harry is gone. Everything that he was dreaming of for his life died the second his head hit that coffee table. And I did that to him."

Sean shakes his head. "It was an accident. You were just horsing around."

Denver's right boot jerks forward another inch. "I try to

tell myself that. Over and over I relive that moment in my mind. And all I think of is that maybe . . . maybe I meant to do it. Maybe I meant to hurt him. He was Mr. Perfect. Always doing the right thing." Denver stares into the valley, his shoulders braced against the rising wind. "Do you have any idea what it's like to live in the shadow of your brother? To live with the guilt that you hurt someone you loved, and may have meant it?"

I do, I think.

I step forward, closer to Sean.

Then I say it. "Denver, I know what that's like. Listen. I killed my best friend." It's the first time I've spoken those words. They cut through me like a newly sharpened blade.

"I didn't mean to, but I . . ." I can't bring myself to describe the scene. What happened. But I force myself to keep talking. "Because of me, he got into an accident and died. He may not have been my brother," I tell Denver, "but he was my best friend." Then the three words that had been battering the inside of my brain for months explode out of my mouth, over and over. "I killed him. I killed him. I killed him."

It was the second-to-last thing on the List.

Despite our fight, we had come so close. Lucas's dad had told us that he would go with us on the trail. Gran gave her consent. We had all the gear, all the maps, everything. We set our start date—August 3. We were prepared.

And then, on a scorching July afternoon exactly a week before we were to hit the trail, we set out to tick off *#9: Jump off the rope swing at the quarry.*

The air was sticky hot as we climbed up to the quarry's edge, humidity clinging to our faces like glue. It had been a brutal summer, the hottest on record. When we reached the rope swing, the muddy water below was the lowest I'd ever seen. It made the rope swing seem even that much higher.

It made me that much more afraid.

But Lucas was never afraid of anything. He peered over the side of the quarry and laughed. "Piece of cake. We'll be swimming around in that nice cool water in no time."

And then Lucas said it. Seven words that have haunted me every single day. "Toe, do you want to go first?"

He had listened to me when I had yelled at him. About always being the follower. He wanted to give me the chance to change that. To prove that I could be a leader, too.

In that moment I wanted more than anything to take charge. To be the one who finished number nine on the List first. But then I took another look down at the water so far below, and I couldn't do it.

"No," I told Lucas. "You go first."

And so Lucas climbed up the tall red oak with the rope swing slung around its thickest branch and soared off with the grace of an angel, swan-diving straight into a block of granite hidden a foot beneath the water's surface.

I slid down the steep quarry walls, screaming his name as I pulled him out of the water. But by the time I got to him, he was unconscious. He had broken his neck. He died an hour later, in the hospital where we had first met.

Sharp explosions of noises snap me out of my memory. Moose is by my side, giving short, sharp warning barks. His yipping pulls me back into the present, reminding me that I can't lose myself to the past when a friend needs help now.

As my eyes refocus, Denver has turned around. He is looking at me. I wait for him to judge me.

Instead, he gives me a look of confusion. Of not knowing what to think.

The whole truth comes spilling out before I can stop it. "I wish it had been me who had died. It should have been me. But it wasn't, and I'm still here." I realize only as I'm saying it that it's true. No matter how guilty and broken I've felt, I haven't given up on Lucas or on myself. No matter how unlucky or dumb I am, I've kept going.

"I made a promise to Lucas that I would hike to Katahdin with him, and I'm going to keep my promise." I am shaking, but standing taller than I've ever stood before.

"You made a mistake, too. But as much as you think your brother must hate you, he wouldn't have wanted you to jump off a cliff. And he's still out there." I swallow a lump in my throat. "You could still work things out with him."

"That's not true," Denver says quietly. "When he lost his eye, when he found out he would never be able to see if a baseball was an inch or a mile from his head for the rest of his life, he told me he wished I were dead. And then he disappeared."

"Screw Harry," Sean says. "Screw his career and his eye and the guilt he put on you."

"I know what it's like to live with so much guilt that . . . that you can barely go on," I say. For a quick second, the past year flashes through my mind, dim and hazy and gray. Taking an ax and destroying the tree house we had built while screaming bloody murder. Not being able to eat a blueberry or see a worm without breaking down into sobs. Lying in Lucas's backyard for hours, numb with memories and grief.

"But here's the thing." I take a step closer to Denver. "We live through it. We survive. And we learn to forgive ourselves."

It is quiet now, off the trail. There is only the gray sky, the rocks and the cliffs, and us.

My words echo through my head, and for the first time, I wonder if I really can fully forgive myself someday.

Denver stands completely still for a moment. His hands are shaking. He takes a step away from the ledge.

And that's when a gust of wind hits him like a wrecking ball square in the chest.

CHAPTER 27

MOOSE HOWLS AS Denver stumbles backward. His arms go wheeling over his head as Sean lunges to grab him. Their hands just miss.

Denver teeters, his arms flailing, his eyes wide with surprise and fear.

And then he falls.

There is the sound of a body scraping against dirt and rock, and then an awful thud. Moose barks frantically as Sean and I scramble to the edge of the cliff.

Denver is twisted up in a heap on a ledge about twenty feet down. He is motionless and his eyes are closed. His face and front are smeared with mud.

Sean yells Denver's name. Nothing.

Sean yells again.

Denver cracks an eye open.

"Ow," he says.

The breath I had been holding comes whooshing out. I know it's wrong, but I start laughing. Big, whooping gasps of relief come snorting out of me. Denver is alive. He is alive.

Denver peers down at himself and untangles his body until he is sitting up, his legs dangling off the narrow shelf that he has miraculously fallen on.

"You okay, man?" asks Sean.

Denver starts moving different parts of his body one by one. After his arms, he does a little chest shake and prods his legs. When he tries to move his foot, he winces. "I did something to my ankle," he says. He touches it and yelps. "I think it might be sprained."

"Anything else hurt?" asks Sean.

Denver completes his self-inspection. "It's just my ankle, I think."

"Don't worry. We'll get you back." Sean goes to his pack and takes out his bear bag rope.

He wraps one end of the rope around a boulder at the top of the cliff. Then he loops the rope around itself every sixteen inches, making little handhold knots.

When he's done, he tosses the rope over the side. It whips down and slaps loose a couple of pebbles next to Denver's shoulder. Sean grabs the rope near the boulder and yanks it, hard. The rope tightens but doesn't snap. Sean walks back over to the cliff's edge. "Denver, can you climb up?"

Denver grabs onto the rope. Using the handhold knots, he pulls himself up three feet, then four and a half feet, then six feet. But when he gets to seven and a half feet he stops. His feet dangle helplessly in the air. With a groan, Denver lowers himself back down to the ledge. His face is white as he looks up at us. "I don't think I can pull myself up to you guys. I can't use my feet to brace myself."

Sean studies the cliff. He is silent for a long moment. "If I went down there, do you think you could piggyback on me while I bring you up?" he finally asks Denver.

"Yeah, I think I could hold on. But I'm no featherweight, Sean."

"You be quiet."

Holding the rope, Sean walks to the edge of the cliff. He turns around and leans back. The rope holds. "Here goes," he says. He takes a step down, bracing his foot against the side of the cliff. Then he takes another. Hand over hand, he starts shimmying down. Right before his head lowers out of sight, I see him stare down with a look of utter terror on his face.

In that moment I realize that Sean has no idea what he's doing. That the way he took control of the situation and told Denver he would rescue him was just a front. He's still a kid, just like me.

The rope sways back and forth as Sean continues his descent. I get on my hands and knees and crawl to the edge of the cliff. When I peer over, Sean is halfway to Denver. His knuckles have turned white from gripping the rope.

"You've got this, buddy," says Denver.

Sean takes another step. His foot slips on a smooth patch of rock. His other foot slides free, and he smashes into the cliff. When he pulls away, a line of blood trickles down from a gash on his cheek.

He doesn't bother trying to put his feet back on the cliff. Instead, he dangles and lowers himself in a panic using just his arms and his hands. His chest slides across a couple of rocks that tumble free. They seem to bounce forever on their way down.

With a gasp, Sean crumples next to Denver. He wraps his hand around the rope and leans forward, his forehead just touching the rock. His shoulders are trembling.

When he moves again, it is to look up at the cliff he is going to have to climb with his best friend on his back. It looks terrifying. But I don't want him to feel my fear, so I give him a thumbs-up.

"All right," Sean says to Denver. "Up you go."

Sean slowly turns to the side and crouches next to Denver. Denver wraps his arms around Sean's neck, balancing on his good foot and wrapping one leg around Sean's waist. With a little hop, he is on Sean's back.

Sean's knees wobble for a moment, but then they hold steady. He looks up. I see his eyes and know he's going to make it. Time stretches out forever as I watch him put one hand above the other, pulling more than three hundred pounds of weight off the ledge. Every time he pulls himself up and brings his arms down to his chest, he wraps the rope around one leg and traps the rope between both his boots, taking the weight off his arms. I understand now why it would have been useless for Denver to try to climb the rope. With a busted ankle, there's no way he could have used Sean's technique to get off the cliff.

Sean starts fast, grunting every once in a while as he powers through, but otherwise there's no sign that he's under any sort of pressure.

But then, two-thirds of the way up, Sean begins to slow down. Even though it's chilly, beads of sweat gather at his temples and roll down his face. He pauses, and suddenly he's breathing fast and short. He is hyperventilating.

"Keep on moving!" I yell to him. Sean's hand slips, and he and Denver drop a foot. Denver reaches out and grabs the rope to try to take some of his weight off Sean. His injured foot brushes against a jutting rock, and he gives a short, sharp yelp.

I reach down, but my hand is still far from where Sean and Denver are. I try to pick up the rope and pull on it, but it doesn't budge. I am no match for the combined weight of two bodies. "Hang on," I yell to them. My palms begin to sweat as I look around desperately for anything that will help.

Sean's trekking poles are lying next to his pack. I grab one of them and run back to the cliff edge. I get on my stomach and lower the pole down. It's just within reach of Sean and Denver. "Denver, grab on!" I say.

Denver shakes his head. "You're half my size. I'd pull you over." He grips the rope and swings himself on the other side of Sean. He starts hauling himself up, using his good foot to push up from the cliff wall.

Sean has stopped climbing. His hands slide an inch. "I don't how much longer I can hang on."

"Don't you give up." I drop the trekking pole and race to my pack. I pull out my bear bag rope, the one that Lucas and I got at a yard sale for three dollars. It's flimsy, but it'll have to do. I fling one end around the boulder next to Sean's rope and tie a square knot to keep it in place. I run back to the cliff edge and tie a bowline around myself.

I wrap the rope around my right leg a few times and get back on the ground. Denver is only a foot from the edge, gasping with effort. I reach down. "I've roped myself to a rock up here," I tell him. "You're not going anywhere." I hope it's true.

Denver reaches up, and I grab his arm. I pull hard while he lets go of the rope and uses his other arm to push-up himself over the cliff edge. His chest flops onto the ground. I shift my grip to both his armpits and drag him until the rest of his body has made it safely over the edge.

Denver is already swiveling on his belly when I let go of him. "Sean!" he yells.

We scramble to the edge.

Sean has slid all the way back down to the ledge. "I don't know if I can make it," he says. He holds up both of his hands. Thick slashes of angry red skin cut across both his palms. "My hands are really messed-up."

"Can you hold on to the rope?" asks Denver.

Sean winces as he tries. "It hurts, but yeah."

"Then hang on." Denver crawls to the boulder where the rope is wrapped. He scuffs out a hole in the dirt with his good foot and braces himself against it. He grabs the rope and begins to pull.

I crouch in front of Denver and begin to pull with him. Coils of rope gather at our feet as we lift Sean up the side of the cliff.

Even with the two of us, it's heavy work. I can't see Denver behind me, but I can hear him grunt under the strain every few seconds. My limbs feel like they are on fire. But we keep pulling, and before long Sean's head crests over the cliff.

Denver's bad ankle thwacks into the dirt and his legs buckle involuntarily. His good foot gives out from under him, smashing into the boulder and twisting at a weird angle.

All of a sudden all of Sean's weight is on me. I clutch the rope desperately, but without Denver's weight, I go sprawling.

My face hits the cliff edge right over Sean, who has slid back three feet.

"Tony, I'm slipping!" Denver says. He is sitting down now, holding on to the boulder with one hand and the rope with the other. Both his feet are useless now.

I see the trekking pole that I had abandoned a few minutes ago. I let go of the rope and grip the pole below the handle and thrust it down. The pointed tip is eye level with Sean. "Grab it!" I scream.

He flings out his arm and grabs the pole. With Sean's weight between the rope and the pole, Denver and I claw him back up to the top of the cliff and onto solid ground.

As we lie there gasping, I stare up at the sky and watch as the gray storm clouds break. Moose trots over to me and begins to lick my face as a slice of blue sky appears, and sunlight glimmers down on us.

I turn on my side. Denver has both eyes closed in pain, but Sean's eyes are bright and open, staring at me. "Thank you," he says. And like a miracle unfolding, he smiles at me.

CHAPTER 28

"SO," SAYS DENVER.

"So," I say.

Denver is tucked in his sleeping bag. He looks like a kid waiting for a bedtime story. After we were all safe, Sean and I had pitched a tent and put him inside. Adrenaline had kept him standing while pulling Sean up the cliff, but once his friend was out of danger, Denver found he couldn't put any weight on either ankle without collapsing in pain.

Sean and I formed a game plan. We had no way of contacting anyone from where we were—I didn't have a phone, and Sean and Denver had left theirs in the glove compartment of Sean's car. Sean would run to Lakes of the Clouds Hut to get a rescue party. I would stay with Denver and make sure he was taken care of until they arrived.

Sean has been gone for half an hour, and now it's my turn to make hot chocolate. Denver instructs me on how to assemble his Jetboil stove. I twist a cylindrical white gas canister into the fuel line, then screw a pot of water onto the top of the stove. There's a little plastic starter that lights the stove with one firm press. With a lid on, the whole pot of water bubbles in about three minutes.

"I gave you my marshmallows," I say when I enter the tent with two steaming mugs. Moose paces outside, before settling down next to the vestibule.

"Thanks." Denver takes the mug brimming with sticky white foam and blows on it gently. "So tell me more about yourself, Tony," he says.

I think for a moment. "Well, first of all, my real name is Toby."

Denver's eyes widen. I can see him adding up in his mind all the lies I've told him. I half expect him to be disgusted by my fibs.

Instead he asks, "Do you really think you can make it all the way to Katahdin?"

I answer honestly. "I don't know. But I have to try."

Denver gives me a long, hard look. "Did you tell your parents you were going?"

I shake my head. "My parents don't care. They're divorced. I live with my grandma." I swallow a mouthful of chocolate. The hot liquid runs down my throat, warming me to my toes. "My mom and dad married really young. They didn't really know what they were doing when I was born. They argued a lot.

"Every couple of months they'd take me to see Gran. She would always greet me on her front porch with a new book and a fun-sized bag of peanut M&M'S. And when she tucked me in at night, she would make the most fantastic bedtime stories, with brave dragons and nasty princes and all sorts of magic spells.

"When my parents finally divorced, neither of them could afford to keep me. Gran took me in. She turned her sewing room into my bedroom and painted it my favorite color, forest green. She made me blueberry pancakes every Saturday."

I smile, remembering. "Last spring, we even tapped the sugar trees in the backyard and made a gallon of maple syrup. Still haven't run out of it yet." My smile falters. "At least, I don't think we've run out."

Denver sets down his mug. "Do you love your grandma?"

"Yes," I say softly.

"Does she know that you're on the trail?"

"I . . . don't know."

"Does she care about you?"

I stare into my mug. All of a sudden the chocolate tastes too sweet. "Yes."

"Don't you think she's worried sick?" Denver asks.

"No," I say. But as the word leaves my mouth, it already feels like a lie. "I left a note."

"And what did you say?"

"That I had to go away for a while. That I would be okay. And not to worry."

"Toby. She's probably scared to pieces right now. How long have you been gone?"

I count in my head. "Eight days."

Denver half sits, resting against his elbows as he drinks his hot chocolate. "You know, when Harry was about your age, he ran away from home. He was gone for only a day, but it was enough to watch my parents go nearly crazy. They called the cops after he had been gone for twelve hours, and were told that Harry would have to be missing for twenty-four hours before they could file a missing-persons report.

"So we went home. And waited. My dad couldn't stop pacing up and down the living room floor. My mom couldn't stop crying. When Harry finally came strolling in eighteen hours and twenty-seven minutes after he had left, he didn't care that he had caused such terror."

Denver leans back in his sleeping bag and closes his eyes. "It's something I had a hard time forgiving him for—for not caring." He looks at me. "It's a terrible thing, to make someone you love worry."

I drop my head. "I'd like to let Gran know that I'm okay, but I don't want to stop hiking. If she finds out where I am, I'll be yanked off the trail faster than you can say *hot popcorn*."

"What if someone were to give her a message saying that you were all right? I could do that."

"You could?"

"Sure. When I get down off the mountain, I'll give her a call. I won't let her know who I am or where I saw you. All I'll say is that you're safe." Denver grins. "You saved my life. It's the least I can do for you."

Denver's cup is empty. I try to take it out of his hands, but he doesn't let go for a moment. "I want to know more about Lucas," he says.

I tug, and the cup comes free. "What about him?" My guard goes up. I'm not sure I want to tell the whole story, even now.

"What's your favorite memory of him?"

That makes me pause. It has been so long since I've thought of Lucas without grief. I think about Denver's question. About Lucas. I can't stop the guilt that floods through me. But for the first time, I wade through it. I rewind past the rope swing, our fights, the morning we made the List, all the way to a day that I had nearly forgotten.

"When I turned nine, Lucas got me a brand-new baseball mitt and bat for my birthday. We went out to my backyard and played for hours. He made up this game where we pretended to be famous Red Sox players—Babe Ruth, Ted Williams, David Ortiz—and spent the afternoon hitting home runs, stealing bases, yelling at our imaginary ump—an old pine tree, chewing gum, and scuffing our feet in front of our home plate, a cut-up placemat from Lucas's kitchen.

"We played until sunset and then went inside, where Gran had made a gigantic chocolate birthday cake with buttercream frosting—my favorite."

I can't help smiling, talking about it. "After that, we always called the tree Ump, and we'd even nail a jersey to him during baseball season every year."

Denver laughs.

"That was the best day of my life," I say. "But then Lucas died." Something catches in my throat. "Ever since I can remember, I've been bad luck to anyone I meet."

Denver shakes his head. "I would say you're just the opposite, Toby. For me, at least."

Now my hot chocolate is gone, too. I take both dirty cups and go outside, rinsing them out before tucking them back into Denver's pack. I put away the stove and feed Moose a couple of cheese blocks and a handful of dog biscuits.

When I get back into the tent, Denver has fallen asleep. Before I curl up in my sleeping bag and let the wind lull me to sleep, I dig out a Ziploc bag from the hidden pocket of my pack's hood. I unzip the top and take out a wrinkled piece of paper. I smooth over the creased lines. Even though I've carried it with me all this way, it's the first time I've been able to bring myself to read it since starting the trail.

#1 Go fishing
#2 Eat a worm
#3 Spend a whole day at the movie theater
#4 Build a tree house
#5 Go blueberry picking
#6 Make a raft and float it
#7 Explore the abandoned house on Chimney Hill
#8 Learn how to pop wheelies on our bikes
#9 Jump off the rope swing at the quarry

#10 Hike the Appalachian Trail from Velvet Rocks to Katahdin

Screw bad luck. I'm going to do it. I'm going to finish the List. For Lucas. And for me.

CHAPTER 29

"KNOCK, KNOCK."

Somebody is tapping at the tent door. The zipper peels down, and I see Abbey's beautiful face hovering over me. "Hey there, kiddo," she says. She is carrying a first aid kit and a small backpack.

I rub my eyes and sit up and run my hands through my hair, yanking through the knots that have gathered. I hope I look dashing. "Wello-there! I mean, hallo well— Well, hello there! What are you doing here?" I bare my teeth in a crazy grin.

Abbey peels the tent flap back even farther, and I see a crowd of people outside.

"I've brought the search-and-rescue team," Abbey says. "Lakes radioed over to Mizpah. We have crew and guests from both huts who heard about your situation and wanted to help."

There is a chorus of hellos and Sean comes into view. His rope-burned hands are swathed in bandages. "How's Denver?" he asks.

Denver lets out a snore.

"I think he's going to be okay," I say. I poke Denver. "Time to get rescued."

Denver opens one eye. "Five more minutes," he mumbles. He closes the eye.

Abbey clears her throat, and Denver opens both eyes. "I mean, I'm ready," he says.

"Move over, Tony," says Abbey. She ducks into the tent and zips up the flap to seal in the heat. "Has he had any painkillers?" she asks me.

I shake my head. Abbey opens the first aid kit and takes out four ibuprofen. She pops them in Denver's mouth and hands him a bottle full of water. "Lie back down," she orders Denver as soon as he has swallowed the pills.

She opens Denver's sleeping bag until his feet are showing. She takes Denver's sock with the tips of her fingers. Very gently, she pulls his sock back, exposing his ankle. She does the same with the other sock.

Denver hisses and bites his lip. "How bad is it, Doc?"

I take a peek. Both Denver's ankles are purple. His right one is swollen to at least twice the size of his left.

"There's no bleeding, which is good." Abbey pinches Denver's big toe. "Can you feel this?"

Denver nods.

Abbey pinches the rest of Denver's toes. Each time he gives a nod when she asks if he can feel it. "How about wiggling your toes?" she asks.

Denver concentrates, and his toes give a little wave.

"Good," says Abbey. "You haven't lost circulation in your feet. Since both your ankles are injured, you're not going to be walking out of here, but we won't need to helicopter you out.

"Hey, Bill!" she calls.

"Yeah?" says a voice from outside the tent.

"Radio front desk. Tell them we're taking the patient up to Washington. He's got two sprained ankles but does not require immediate evacuation. We'll radio when we're at Lakes and give an ETA on our arrival. If the weather holds, it shouldn't take us more than two or three hours to get from Lakes to the top of Washington."

I know that Lakes is only one mile below the summit. A normal hiker would need less than an hour to reach the top of Washington from the hut. Carrying Denver out is going to be a slow task.

"Will do, Captain," says Bill.

Abbey turns her attention back to Denver. "I'm going to make a U-splint for your ankles." She opens her backpack and takes out a T-shirt. She rolls it into a long, tight tube. "Hold this," she tells me.

My fingers brush hers as she gives me the T-shirt. I am the luckiest kid in the world.

Abbey puts her hands around Denver's ankle and carefully turns his foot until it's at a ninety-degree angle to his shin. "Wrap the center of the T-shirt around the sole of his foot. Then put both the ends of the shirt along the sides of his leg and hold them there," she tells me.

I do as I'm instructed. It feels good to have someone who knows what she's doing. Abbey lets go of Denver's foot and reaches for a roll of tape in the med kit. She starts taping the ball of the foot, then wraps around the T-shirt and the rest of the foot, over the ankle, and up the side of the leg. When she is done, the T-shirt and the tape are holding Denver's ankle firmly in place.

Abbey adds two more layers of tape before she is satisfied with her work. Then she does the same thing with the second ankle. "Now you are going to scoot yourself to the tent entrance, and folks are going to pick you up and bring you into the sleeping bag on the litter outside. After that, we will be carrying you out."

Denver sits up and gives a little salute. "Aye, aye, Captain."

Abbey opens the tent, and Denver skooches himself to the entrance. A couple of hands reach down and lift him up, then swing him onto a bright orange sled with a puffy blue sleeping bag laid open on it.

Denver lies down, and Abbey zips up the bag. She jams a hat onto Denver's head. "Lie back and relax," she says. "You've got a ways to go."

Abbey counts off a dozen people, then instructs numbers one through six to gather around the litter. Number one is at the head, number four is at the rear, and two, three, five, and six are along the sides. On the count of three, they lift the litter and begin to carry Denver. The others follow behind, ready to switch off whenever the team gets tired.

As the litter carry makes its way slowly over the rough ground, Sean stays with me while I pack the tent away. Once we've made sure we haven't forgotten anything, we catch up to the rescue operation just as they are getting back on the trail.

The rain comes again in a sudden fury. It doesn't turn to hail, but a vicious wind starts up. Everyone pauses and breaks out waterproof coats before continuing on. By the time the roof of Lakes of the Clouds comes into view, the temperature has dropped about twenty degrees and the rocks on the trail are starting to ice over.

When we clomp into the hut, icy raindrops scattering everywhere, Abbey has the rescue team set Denver down in the foyer next to the dining room. She checks Denver's ankles again. "Looks like you've still got circulation in your feet. The weather's too dangerous to go any farther tonight. How do you feel about spending the night here and heading to the top of Washington tomorrow morning? If the weather's all right and the auto road is opened, your parents can drive up and meet you there."

"I think the ibuprofen is working, and I'm feeling rather comfy. And I'd rather spend the next ten hours in a hut instead of getting pummeled by the weather," says Denver.

"Hey, Nate!" Abbey calls to one of the Lakes crew members. "Any free bunks tonight?"

Nate nods toward a long, narrow corridor with doors on either side. "We've got one left. I checked right before dinner. There's a free bottom bunk in the third bunkroom down that he can take."

Abbey directs the litter-carry to heave Denver up one more time. We walk past the tables packed with hut guests about to dig into their soup, down the hallway, and turn into a bunkroom. Abbey has the litter placed next to a bottom bunk bed with three neatly folded woolen blankets on it.

The search-and-rescue volunteers and the rest of the hut crew go back to the dining room to eat, leaving Sean, Abbey, and me with Denver.

Abbey hoists Denver out of the drenched search-and-rescue sleeping bag and onto the mattress. She checks his feet one last time. "With some RICE, you should be all set," she tells him.

"I was just thinking I was kind of hungry," said Denver.

Abbey cracks a smile. "RICE is an acronym. It stands for 'rest, ice, compression, elevation.' It's standard procedure for sprains and strains." She takes a few extra blankets that are on a bench near the door and tucks them under Denver's feet.

She digs into the med kit one more time and breaks out a couple of instant ice packs. She whacks them against the floor to activate them, then drapes them around Denver's ankles. "Rest," she says. "I'll be back soon with soup."

Denver lies back and closes his eyes. "Hey, guys," he says.

"Yeah?" says Sean.

"Thank you."

"Get some sleep, buddy." Sean nods toward the door. He and I tiptoe out as Denver begins to snore again.

CHAPTER 30

THE WEATHER'S SO horrible that Sean and I don't even think about heading out to set up our tents. We find the Lakes crew in the kitchen and the guy named Nate shows us an extra bunkroom called the Dungeon. The door is rusty, with badly peeling turquoise paint and a wooden sign that reads "REFUGE ROOM—EMERGENCY USE ONLY" in wind-battered red letters.

"This is our emergency shelter. It's designed to take an overflow of hikers in bad weather. We're full up now, but you guys can stay here for tonight," says Nate.

I'm glad I'm not sleeping inside the hut. Even though I thought there had been way too many people in Zealand two days ago, it's nothing compared to the hordes of people inside Lakes. I read somewhere that the hut can hold over a hundred people. Definitely a number I am not comfortable with. I put my hand on the Dungeon door and push it open.

Inside, half a dozen wooden bunk beds form an L-shape in the corner farthest from the door. It is a basic setup, chilly, but blocked from the rain and the wind.

Moose sniffs around our place for the night while Sean and I lay our sleeping pads and bags on the two bottom bunks. It's creepy down here. I begin to notice the constant low moan of the wind. The cold and the damp. The feeling of being on a mountain, far from civilization. I can see why it is called the Dungeon.

Once we've set up our bunks, Sean and I return to the hut for dinner. We eat quickly, I let Moose outside for a minute, and then we return to the Dungeon for the night. We don't get much sleep. Moose paces the cold stone floor of the Dungeon, his nails clicking restlessly.

The next morning Abbey and the two other crew members from Mizpah head back over the ridge to their hut. Abbey gives me a hug before she leaves. "Denver told me everything. They were lucky to have you there."

My cheeks turn to fire.

"Take care, Tony," Abbey says. She heads toward the door.

"It's Toby," I say.

But she's already gone.

Nate takes over the rescue operation. Denver's ankles have gotten a little better during the night, but he still can't walk. After breakfast, Nate gathers a dozen volunteers and loads Denver back up in the litter.

The wind is blowing steadily when we leave the hut, but the skies are clear. The morning forecast calls for sun for the next couple of hours. For the litter-carry, it is a warm, easy walk along the gentle boulder-strewn path. Moose trots next to me, even when I'm taking a turn carrying Denver.

I see the buildings on top of Washington before the actual summit. Metal towers that resemble rocket launchers rise up in the air. The elevated trestle of the Cog Railway rises up underneath a single locomotive belching out coal-black smoke as it pulls a trainload of tourists up the mountain.

We crest a rocky hill, and suddenly we are standing at the edge of a round stone tower. It looks like something Rapunzel would have lived in. There is a humungous parking lot filled with opening and closing car doors. Swarms of people are walking up a set of wooden stairs toward the true summit. Some are wearing packs and using trekking poles, but many of them are in thin cotton shirts, with big cameras strapped around their necks, shuffling in loafers or clutching purses. If a sudden gale struck up, they would be Popsicles.

"Larry. Larry! Look at that, Larry!" A woman with bright pink lips and a thick Jersey accent elbows the hairy arm of a lumbering man with a waxed head that shines like a newly mopped kitchen floor.

"Quit your poking, Janice!" says Larry.

"There's a body in that sled. Ooh, take a picture for the kids!" Janice hustles over to us. Larry wobbles behind.

A dozen heads turn, and we are set upon by a mob of tourist photographers. There's a guy with a heavy-duty Nikon, crouching down to take low-angled pictures. Two ladies in matching pink miniskirts and bejeweled sandals, each of them holding their iPhones sideways as they walk toward us. A girl with one of those old-school disposable cameras that still uses film. Larry hobbles to the front and starts taking pictures of the litter. Moose growls, and I put my hand on his head to calm him.

"Everyone, step back," shouts Nate. "This is a rescue operation, not a circus show."

"Ooh, how bad is it? Is he dead?" asks Janice. "Larry, take a picture of the dead guy!"

"Sir!" yells Nate. His voice drops an octave. "Step away from the litter!"

"Let me just get this shot." Larry leans over to take a picture of Denver's face.

I glance at Sean. His hands are clenched. He looks about ready to punch Larry in the face.

"Sir!" Nate barks again. "If you do not remove yourself immediately from the situation, I am going to call the Fish and Game warden and have you detained for obstructing a rescue operation."

"There's no such thing as that." Larry clicks away.

"You are violating park service code seven-twelve-oh-one-two, whereby any citizen who deliberately ignores a search-and-rescue leader is subject to a five-thousand-dollar fine. Do you want me to call and make that official?" Nate removes his walkie-talkie from his belt and holds it up to his ear.

"All right, all right," Larry grumbles. He moves to the side and lets the litter pass.

▲▲

"Larry, check the pictures, make sure they're good," says Janice. "I want to show Mavis and Jerry that we saw a real dead guy."

With a few more threats, Nate clears the crowd so the litter can move up a series of wooden steps to a huge bunker-like visitor center at the top.

I tell Moose to stay outside and take a final turn helping to carry Denver into the building. I look down and realize why Janice thought he was dead. Through the whole scene, Denver has been fast asleep.

Once we are settled in the visitor center, Nate calls Denver's parents, who are driving up an auto road to the summit.

Nate hangs up the phone. "Your folks will be here in about half an hour," he tells Denver.

"Hey, Nate," I say.

"Yeah?"

"Could you really have gotten that guy arrested and fined?"

Nate laughs. "Nope."

"But what about that code?"

"I'm hut crew. My job is to make up official-sounding stuff."

Nate unzips Denver's sleeping bag. "Time for one more ankle check before I send you on your way."

As Nate starts his final inspection, the smell of fried food suddenly hits me. After weeks of being on the trail, the scent is enough to lure me away from Denver and Sean and to the visitor center's cafeteria. It is bustling with hungry tourists, some in high heels, tottering around looking for hot chocolate or bowls of clam chowder, hot dogs wrinkled with overheating, burgers flipped in lard, and big, fat, wonderful french fries.

I buy a tray of fries and douse them in ketchup. As I munch on them, I take a better look around. Next to the cafeteria there is a souvenir shop that sells key chains, THIS CAR CLIMBED MOUNT WASHINGTON bumper stickers, chocolate-covered almonds posing as "Moose Poop," T-shirts and sweatshirts and hats and bandannas.

It is too much. As good as the fries taste, I'm ready to be back outside, away from civilization. I return to Denver and Sean. "Hey, guys, I think I'll get going."

Denver sits up and reaches into his pocket. He takes a piece of paper and a pen. "Well?" he says. He looks at me expectantly. "Am I going to get your grandma's number or not?"

That's right. I hesitate, but I know that Denver wouldn't betray my trust. He will get Gran a message without having her try to stop what I need to do. I tell him the number.

Denver writes down the digits and tucks the paper in his pocket.

"Hey," says Sean. He crosses over to me. Before I know what's happening, I'm wrapped up in a fierce hug. I stand there, paralyzed. My mind can't believe that gruff-and-tough Sean would actually do something like this. Then, without thinking, I hug him back.

Sean lets go of me and uses the back of his hand to rub away something in his eye. "I know I was rotten to you when we met, but I'm really glad we found you."

"I'm glad we found one another." I mean it. By some stroke of incredible luck, we helped to save one another from the past. Denver from his brother, me from Lucas. A wave of sadness hits me. I realize that I probably won't ever see these guys again. I open my mouth. I want to tell them how awesome they are, and that I'm going to miss them, and that now that they have Gran's number maybe they could call sometime and we could catch up.

But then out of the corner of my eye I see a man with Denver's blue eyes and a woman with his dark-brown hair rushing toward us, and I know I have to get going before they start asking me questions. "I gotta go," I mumble, and lunge for my backpack.

"Bye, kid," says Sean.

"Safe travels, Toby," says Denver.

"Thanks. You get home safe, too."

I hitch up my pack and head out, just missing Denver's parents as they barrel toward their son. I call to Moose, and within a few seconds, we are on our way. It is a relief to hurry off the top of Washington and make for Mount Jefferson, the next peak over. The crowds fade into straggles of people once I start climbing across the ridge, away from the parking lot and train stop.

The top of Jefferson is a small outcropping of rocks. I clamber up it, and as I stare at the metal geological marker marking the top, it occurs to me that I didn't actually touch the true summit of Washington. It would have been the highest point for me on the entire trail.

A moment later, it also occurs to me that it doesn't matter. I doesn't matter that I got within a hundred feet of the summit and forgot to actually touch it. I saved a guy from jumping off a cliff. I've got a lucky marble in my pack. I fed a dog, who saved me from a moose. I'm doing all right.

After a snack of tortillas and cheese for Moose and me, it is time to move on. We tackle Mount Adams next, then descend down.

The top of Madison is less than half a mile up. When I reach it, it's getting to be late afternoon. Three miles later, we are at Osgood tentsite—our stopping point for the night. We've hiked over four peaks and gone ten miles today, one of them being Denver's three-hour carryout. Not too bad.

I take out my stove and coax a round blue flame to life. I fill my pot halfway with water and set it on the stove. As the water forms tight bubbles around the edge of the pot, I peel the cardboard tab back on the rice-and-beans box and pull open the plastic sack inside.

I pour the rice and beans in the boiling water and turn the flame down to low, letting it simmer while I cut pieces of sausage and drop them into the pot. Just before the soupy mixture is done, I push a slab of cheese into the center and let it melt into a core of gooey goodness.

I twist the fuel knob until the flame dies and lift the pot off the stove. I let it sit for a few minutes with the cover on, then settle it and myself on a large flat rock to eat my dinner. I hear clicking toenails, and Moose jumps up on the rock beside me. I ruffle his head and pour some of my food out for him to lap up.

After dinner, I pitch my tent and then sit outside to watch the sunset.

Golden streaks lace the sky before the midnight blue of dark creeps down. The sun drops below the horizon, and already a half-moon is dimly visible. There is something calming about this sunset. It doesn't mean a night of uncertainty and cold, or aloneness.

Moose pads up beside me and flops down. His head rests on my knee, and together we watch the stars come out.

CHAPTER 31

THE NEXT MORNING, Moose and I set off for Carter Notch Hut eleven miles away. I don't intend on spending the night there, but I do have to return Andy's lucky marble to the crew. I figure that it has gotten me this far—I can do the rest of the trail alone. Plus, I can ask the crew if they know any stealth sites where I can camp. The next shelter past Carter is another seven miles, and even though I'm feeling pretty good, eighteen miles is still way too much for me to attempt to hike in a day.

Moose and I tread carefully down a steep section of trail, but once we reach the bottom of the valley there is nothing but smooth, flat going for miles.

My stride feels longer; my heart feels stronger. There is a toughness that is beginning to take root in my body. I can feel it in the way I move, how my steps are firmer, the swing of my trekking poles rhythmic and sure.

We reach the Pinkham Notch visitor center in the early afternoon. Inside is a dining room and a store that sells gloves, hats, maps, water-filtration systems, hand and toe warmers.

There is a topographic model of the mountains and valleys in the area, with trails marked in little dotted red lines.

I follow signs for the bathrooms down a flight of steps and discover that there are coin-operated showers available. I go to the front desk and get a handful of quarters as well as a clean towel for two dollars. I pay with a twenty and as I'm waiting for change, I double-check my money Ziploc. I've got one hundred and eighty two dollars left.

I return to the showers and go into a stall. After peeling off my clothes, I slide a quarter into the coin slot on the wall and twist a knob. As soon as the hot water hits my skin, I know I've made the right decision. I groan with happiness and am very glad that there is no one in the bathroom to hear me. I get to work scrubbing, getting in between each finger- and toenail, the spaces behind my ears, every corner of my armpits, every inch of my scalp. Each quarter buys me three minutes of time, and I go through three full dollars before I reluctantly let the water shut off.

I dry myself and rub the towel hard against my wet hair until it sticks up in half-dried knots. Even though I'm getting back into dirty clothes, when I leave the bathroom I feel like a million bucks.

After refilling my water bottles and returning the towel, I stop by the dining room for a sandwich and some lemonade. By the time I start back on the trail, I'm nearly running with new energy.

After miles of downhill or flat, the trail turns abruptly to loose, steep rock. Moose finds his own way through the dense brush, popping out every once in a while to make sure I am still there.

Up, up, up. Sweat rolls down my temples. My shirt is drenched and rubs against my skin where my backpack straps are pressed. My hip belt begins to feel like a sticky octopus tentacle, clinging to my waist as the weight of my pack digs into the small of my back.

But despite all this, I'm not uncomfortable. My lungs are working hard, and my pulse is high, but steady and even. Each rock scramble is a little puzzle, solvable with a couple of pulled tree roots and well-placed boot steps.

The small, stony Carter Notch Hut comes into view by early evening. I figure I'll go inside when it's darker and drop off Andy's marble, then find a place to camp a little farther away.

I continue down the trail. I come to a couple of small lakes and walk halfway around one before setting myself down for a little snack before dinner. I open my pack and dig out a granola bar. I break off a chunk and give it to Moose, then sit and munch as I watch ripples roll calmly over the lake. I've hiked eleven miles today, in some of the most rugged sections of the entire Appalachian Trail. I feel good and fine and happy.

"Lucas, buddy, I wish you were with me." The words appear out of nowhere.

I wait for the guilt to come on, as it always does. But then something miraculous happens. It takes me a moment to realize what it is.

I feel happy.

Somehow, through the mess of it all, I feel like Lucas is here with me. Telling me that he is proud of me for standing on my own two feet. For being able to go on without him.

Maybe I'm not a screwup after all. Maybe my bad luck is finally going away.

There is a rustling behind me, and Moose barks a warning. I turn to see an enormous black raven jabbing its head into my pack.

"Shoo!" I cry as I leap to my feet.

The raven jerks back, and my heart drops. In its beak is Andy's lucky marble.

"No!" I shout. I lunge toward the thief. But it is too late. The raven takes off into the thick woods beyond the lake, with Moose right behind.

I race after them—straight into a thicket of dense bramble bushes studded with thorns. By the time I pull myself free, my arms are covered in scratches and both Moose and the bird thief have disappeared.

When Moose finally circles back to me, he looks disappointed. There is no raven in his mouth. There is no marble, either.

I don't know what to do. I sink to my knees and close my eyes. I totally jinxed myself. It was foolish for me to believe that bad luck wouldn't follow me wherever I went.

I stay kneeling until Moose starts nudging me with his nose. I can't just stay here. I get up and return to the lake.

It's getting on dinnertime, but I'm not hungry. I don't want to go inside the hut and face the crew.

I could pretend that I was never given the marble. It's cowardly, and wrong. But I could do it. Go on my way. Stay on the trail and keep my promise to Lucas. I never asked to be in charge of something that important, anyway.

I take a deep breath. I accept that I'm a coward. I'd rather run away in the dark instead of face the crew at Carter and tell them that I lost Andy's great-grandfather's marble. The one that kept him alive during WWII.

Moose whines uncertainly as I sling my pack on my back. "Let's go, Moose," I say shortly. By the time we get to the next shelter, it will be night. I will have broken my promise to not get caught in the dark. But I tell myself that I don't care.

All the energy from earlier in the day seems to have left my body. My boots feel leaden. It's as if I gain a pound with every step.

I am slowing down, and in my mind I know that I can't do this.

I get a mile out before my feet come to a complete stop. I think about what I told Sean when he asked me why I was on the trail.

"So this is what it feels like to grow up," I whisper in the thickening dark. I take out my headlamp and turn around. I head back toward the hut to accept the consequences.

As I near Carter, something glints at the edge of the trail. I hurry closer.

When I look down, Andy's lucky marble is at my feet.

CHAPTER 32

IN CARTER NOTCH Hut, I give the cook Andy's lucky marble. I feel a twinge of nervousness as the marble drops from my hand into the cook's open palm. From now on, I'm going to have to create all my good luck myself.

The cook invites me to spend the night in one of the bunkhouses, but I tell him that I'm fine. He directs me to a stealth site half a mile farther down the trail, where I set up camp. That night, I let Moose into the tent. I keep my arm around him until he falls asleep.

The next morning I pack up early and head out. It's another 275 miles to the top of Katahdin. I have been on the trail for eleven days. I have forty days left before school starts. Before I've told Gran I would be back.

Plenty of time to make it.

Getting on late afternoon, I meet a southbound thru-hiker named Washboard. He's got a gnarly heap of dread-locks piled around his head, and his shirt is nowhere to be seen. His stomach ripples every time he moves. It's easy to see how he got his name.

Washboard looks me over. "You got some rough stuff ahead of you, man. You ever hear of the killer mile?"

"The killer mile?" I scoff. I'm about to tell Washboard that I've already gone a hundred miles, over the wind and hail of Washington, and I can handle myself, thank you very much, but then I catch a closer look at Washboard's bare skin. It is covered is scrapes and scratches. It looks like a panther tore up his right side. I shiver. Washboard looks like a hard-core hiker. It must have taken some nasty trail for him to get so beat-up.

"They call it the hardest mile on the whole AT. Took me an hour and a half to get through it." Washboard shakes his head. "Man, I'm glad I'm done with that piece."

"How far up ahead is it for me?" I ask.

"Oh, I would say about thirty miles. When you see a peeling birch tree with two banged-in trail signs, one that says something about Goose and another that's got Speck on it, that's when you'll know that the trail is about to get real hairy."

Washboard points to the scratches on his belly. "I got these scrambling over boulders." He turns and shows me a long line of scrapes down the right side of his back. "And I got these scrambling under boulders. And these," he says, turning back around and pointing downward, "are from tripping over all the roots on the ground." It looks like a few baseball bats went swinging at his knees. They are covered in dark, angry purple bruises.

I thank Washboard for the warning and continue on my way. The weather is hot and fine, and my legs carry me over thirteen miles and seven peaks before I make camp at the Rattle River Shelter for the night. As the sun sinks I boil up some pasta and fork the noodles down as I spread open a trail map of northern New Hampshire and Maine.

If I keep going at my pace, we'll be in Maine in a day or two and at the top of Katahdin in three weeks.

"You and me, we're gonna make it," I tell Moose.

Moose woofs. That night, my aloneness feels different from the first few days when I went on the trail. I have a dog outside protecting me. I am no longer a starving, clueless kid.

"Hey, Lucas," I whisper into the quiet of the tent and the stars above my head. I can feel him smiling down at me. "I'm doing it, buddy." I fall asleep to the sound of crickets chirping and the rustle of the wind through the trees.

The next morning I wake up to quiet. I make a bowl of oatmeal and swirl a couple of spoonfuls of peanut butter into it. Moose wags his tail expectantly, and I plop out some of the nutty oatmeal for him. Moose laps up the oatmeal and is still looking at me with hungry eyes, so I dig into my pack and feed him the last of the dog biscuits I had gotten at Lonesome Lake. He wolfs them down, finishing off the last crumb.

Once Moose is fed, it is time to go. After cleaning my cookware in the nearby river, I refill my water bottles, wipe them dry on my shirt, poke my sleeping bag back in its stuff sack, deflate my sleeping pad, and push them into my pack. I break down the tent and lash it to the outside of my pack. I call to Moose, and we are off.

In less than an hour we reach a road. I pull out my map. It's Route 2. About two miles west is the town of Gorham. I know from the lightness of my pack that I need to resupply.

Moose and I walk along the real road into Gorham. I tell him to stay outside as I enter a Cumberland Farms gas station. Inside, I grab energy bars, pasta, and boxes of rice and beans, as well as a three-pound bag of M&M'S. I find the pet aisle and stock up on a ten-pound bag of Purina for Moose. I also get trail maps for Maine. The map Andy had given me only covered New Hampshire.

At the register, I unroll three twenties. As the cashier hands me my change of sixty-seven cents, I study a plastic March of Dimes donation box on the counter. With so much food weight, I'm trying to figure out if the coin weight is worth it.

I realize that I'm thinking about weight this way. A small curl of pride courses through me. I'm thinking like Wingin' It. I'm thinking like a thru-hiker.

I drop the coins in the donation box and head outside. With my pack full and heavy, I pick up Moose and we return to the trail. Despite the weight, I hike another thirteen miles before setting up camp at a shelter. I'm doing great.

The next day, the trail climbs through thick spruce forests, and I pass the sign that Washboard told me about. Soon the trail is choked with boulders. Some of the rocks are as big as houses. We're descending into Mahoosuc Notch. The killer mile.

The temperature drops about twenty degrees. Even in July, there are patches of ice tucked in corners underneath freezing rocks. Broken rocks scatter at my feet, as if giants had been hurling them like snowballs. Fallen trees lie with their mud-encrusted roots fanning out to form humps of writhing earthworms and rotting bark.

It is creepy here. Even the birds seem to have abandoned the place, choosing the warmer temperatures above the notch.

The trail narrows until it is just a waterfall of fallen boulders. When a thick brown arrow marking the path points under a stack of looming rocks, I think about Washboard and his scrapes and bruises.

Mist descends on us, thick and cloudy as milk. Granite cliffs rise above. I feel like I'm gradually being squeezed between a rock giant's hands.

I squirm between two boulders the size of cars. My pack scrapes along the sides, and a water bottle clunks onto the ground, dislodged by the rocks. I pick it up and stuff it deep into the side pocket. After it does it a second time, I stop to mash both bottles inside my pack.

The trail sprouts jagged blades of rock that become more and more difficult to navigate. Moose keeps trotting forward, then dancing back, running into me over and over again. Sometimes I have to pick him up and carry him over slick, steep boulders. I'm not very good at it, and more than once I almost drop him. Even though I've built up a lot of strength on the trail, Moose has been getting heavier. I'm sure I've been feeding him far more than his previous owner. Plus, all the gas station food and all my gear have made my pack bulky. It scrapes against the rocks at every turn.

It takes me and Moose three hours to get through the one mile of the notch. After the ups and downs, the trail turns into marshes and bogs, with nowhere dry to set down a tent. The last glimmers of sunset are fading by the time I reach a shelter.

The next day, the trail spills into an empty parking lot. I pour out some Purina for Moose, and he wolfs it down. As I devour a Snickers and reach for a water bottle, I realize that I have only two mouthfuls of liquid left.

There is a river next to the road. I fill up on water and root around my hood pocket for my iodine pills.

I can't find them.

I pull everything out, checking and rechecking and triple-checking. They are not there.

That nagging voice of doubt that I thought I had conquered on top of Washington is suddenly back. *Did you really think you would be rid of your rotten luck?* it whispers to me. *Of course you would lose them.*

I try to ignore the voice. At least I'm by a road, where I can hitchhike into a town and get another bottle of iodine pills. I pull out my map and check. I shove everything back into my pack and stick my thumb out.

CHAPTER 33

FOUR HOURS LATER, I realize how dumb I was to believe it would be easy to hitch. According to my map, the stretch of road where I'm trying to thumb a lift is ten miles from the nearest town. Only three cars have passed, and none have stopped for a scruffy-looking twelve-year-old standing next to a huge battered backpack and a scrawny dog.

Another hour passes.

It's nearly evening, and I'm just about ready to give up when a car roars up. It is black and shiny and expensive-looking. The windows are tinted.

The window on the driver's side rolls down. A middle-aged man with greased-back gray hair turns his head toward me in the dimming light. He is wearing reflective sunglasses. I can't see his eyes. "Hey, kid," he says. "You want a ride?"

There is something funny about the way he is saying his words. They are thick and sloppy, like an oil slick. Moose barks once. Then again, loudly. This time, I can hear the warning in his voice.

"Come here, kid," says the driver. He pulls his sunglasses away. His eyes look strange and very bloodshot.

I don't know what to do. I could accept a ride with this stranger. I may not like the way he looks, but I need the iodine pills.

The man crooks his finger at me. "Kid. Come. Here." His voice is commanding. Hypnotic.

I walk to the car. Up close, I can see the sweat stains under his button-up shirt. His teeth are yellow. There is a smell coming from him, old tobacco smoke and something else. No one else is in the car with him.

"I want you to get into the car. Right now." The man glares at me. His hand reaches for the door handle.

It hits me. Booze. The man smells like booze.

Moose barks crazily as I step back. The man opens the door as I turn around and run. I reach my pack and for one moment my hand goes down to scoop it up. It is my lifeline in the woods.

But then the man is behind me and closing in fast. Moose jumps in front of him, growling, his teeth bared. The man curses. And then he kicks Moose in the side. Hard.

Moose yelps and stumbles back to me.

I abandon my pack and pick up Moose. Holding my dog to my chest, I run full tilt into the darkening woods.

"Kid! Kid!" screams the man.

I ignore him and scramble into a thicket of scratchy briars. They dig into my pants, but I pull free and keep running.

I am not on the trail. I am trying to get lost somewhere in the forest.

The man's voice fades, then goes away completely. I slow down, panting, listening for him. Nothing. Moose is trembling in my arms.

I see a felled tree trunk lying across the way. It is a huge beech tree with its branches spreading out like angel wings. I gently place Moose under the tree and wriggle beside him.

"Don't bark, Moose," I whisper to him. "Don't make a noise. It's gonna be okay, boy."

We lie there, frozen, until the last of sunset fades through the trees and nighttime blankets the woods in a protective dark. Only then do I dare to move.

There is no sign of the man. No hint of flashlight, no footsteps, nothing. I am safe.

I pick up Moose again and try to retrace my steps. But as the night grows deeper, I realize that I have no idea where I am.

A twig breaks behind me, and my heart explodes with fear. I begin to run blindly, tripping over unseen rocks and roots. It isn't until I smash into a tree and Moose whimpers that I realize I cannot panic.

I stop. In the utter dark, I realize something. Moose depends on me. And right now, in this moment, I need to depend on myself. For us. I can't huddle into my sleeping bag and feel sorry for myself. I have to get us out of this.

"Think, Toby. Think," I say to myself. "What do you need to do to stay alive?"

I have no food. I have no water. I have no tent. There is no wooden shelter to protect me. It is full-on dark. I've completely failed my keeps list.

But there is that tree. And a rising moon that is softly illuminating the forest.

I can keep warm.

In the pale ghostly light, I make my way back to the dead beech. I scrape together a pile of leaves and push them against the trunk, then put Moose inside and shuffle in next to him. I curl into a tight ball around my dog.

The leaves rustle and shift, covering me. Me and Moose aren't exactly comfortable, and I don't get a lot of sleep. But when the pale streaks of dawn come, we are still very much alive.

CHAPTER 34

BY MORNING, MOOSE'S side is swollen and tender, but he is able to walk. Dawn gives way to a leaden sky as we make our way back toward the road, toward my pack and the supplies in it. In daylight it is a little bit easier to see my tracks. I can see where I had fled off the trail and through the thick brush. But when I finally get back to the real road, what I see makes me so angry, I could spit.

My pack has been ripped open and emptied, its contents scattered across the road. My sleeping bag is half out of its stuff sack. When I pick it up, it is heavy. It has been zipped up and filled with dirt and stones. My pad is next to it, an ugly gash slashed into its side.

Lucas's Stansport tent lies like a wounded bird, flapping sadly, wrapped around a tree trunk. I run my hands over it, searching for holes and rips, but the nylon and zippers have withstood the fury of their attack. The tent poles, however, are bent at crazy angles or broken. I wrap the poles in the tent like a shroud. Even though it is most likely beyond repair, I'm not letting go of it.

I find my cookware and headlamp flung wide but unharmed. My first aid kit has been unzipped, the Band-Aids ripped in half, gauze and tape and scissors and bandages missing.

My maps have been torn to pieces. I only know because I find bits of them fluttering in the low branches of a few young maple trees next to the road. The backpack itself has tire marks on it, as though it has been backed up on and run over. It is damaged and dirty, but there are no gaping holes that would make it useless.

Every single bit of brand-new food that I just bought has been opened and dumped and stamped into the dirt. Birds are pecking away at grains of rice on the tar. I see a squirrel make off with a bit of Snickers.

And then I see it. My iodine bottle. I must have not searched for it hard enough. Only now the bottle is in a thousand pieces, smashed against a rock. There are no pills among the shattered glass. The man must have emptied the bottle before destroying it.

I don't cry. Instead, I collect the bits of food that are salvageable—a few energy bars, mangled, but still edible. A handful of M&M'S. I carve away the smears of dirt on a block of cheese and eat the rest of it for breakfast, along with a nearly intact bagel that had been thrown into the brush.

I empty my sleeping bag and brush it out as best I can. I gather up my ripped and scattered belongings and put everything I can find neatly and quickly back into my pack. I check the hidden pocket inside the hood and breathe a small sigh of relief. My Ziploc full of money is still there. So is the List. The man must have not noticed the inner pocket in the dark.

I have to make a decision. I remember the lines and the mileage from studying the map the night before. I can make my way thirty-four more miles down the trail to the next real road. From there, it is only a few miles to the town of Rangeley. I can walk there to restock. Or I can try again to hitchhike from where I am.

Both options are terrible. I am in trouble. But I don't let myself panic. The past few days on the trail have taught me better. If I hiked, I would be in danger of running out of food. I'd have to plan things out carefully. Really test my ability to survive. To be in the woods, alone and hungry.

But then I think about those dark sunglasses, the sharp rotten stench of liquor, and I know I can't expose myself for ten miles down that stretch of road. I'd rather stick to the challenges of the trail than risk running into that man again.

I pick up my pack. "C'mon, Moose," I say, and head down the trail.

I walk steadily and carefully, conserving my energy. I run through my little stockpile of food in my head, calculating and recalculating how much I can eat over the next three days when I will run into another, hopefully friendlier road. I have about thirty miles to go on some candy bar bits and a small cluster of mud-covered M&M'S.

The first day, I eat my remaining food in spare bites. I can only give Moose half an energy bar, but he seems to understand and doesn't beg for more. For lunch, I break out my stove and boil water. It's the only way I can sterilize it now. I pretend it's hot chocolate as I drink it. Hot chocolate loaded with gigantic fluffy marshmallows.

My stomach howls.

Thunder grumbles and threatens, but the rain doesn't come until late afternoon. We have been hiking since dawn, and by that time I have found the shelter. I use the broom in the shelter to sweep out the encrusted dirt in my sleeping bag and settle in for the night. By my calculation, I have only eighteen miles left to go.

Moose and I pass no one on the trail.

The next day I awake to thick, pounding rain. It is cold and heavy, and by the time I finish my meager breakfast of hot water and the last of my M&M'S, it has grown to a full-on lightning and thunderstorm. It is the first time that I've thought the phrase "rain coming down in sheets" and realized it could be so true.

I can't hike in this weather. I don't have enough food to keep me warm. I am eighteen miles from the road up ahead and sixteen miles from the horrible road behind me.

I decide to wait until the weather gets better. In the meantime, I open my water bottles and prop them up on a rock outside so they can catch the rainwater. I have no iodine and will need to capture as much rain as I can. And if it doesn't rain for a while and I run out, I'll need to boil it. And if my fuel runs out, I'll have to risk it with untreated pond water.

After setting my bottles outside, I return to the shelter and huddle in my sleeping bag with Moose. I boil more hot water, sipping it in slow gulps, conserving my energy. I watch as the rain and wind lash at the trees, painting dark streaks across their bark.

By the time the sky finally clears, it is early afternoon and I am down to half a Snickers bar and my fuel canister is rattling toward empty. I have no more food for Moose. As I pack up for my eighteen-mile hike, I hesitate when I spot the battered, useless tent. Lucas's tent.

I should leave it. It is unnecessary weight. Dangerous weight, even. I could collapse from lack of food if I'm not careful. A day of carrying an extra six pounds of nylon and broken poles is like losing at least two Snickers bars' worth of calories.

I place the broken poles in the middle of the tent and roll it up. As I put the tent in my pack, I feel like my promise to Lucas, to finish the trail, is wrapped up with it. The tent is heavy.

But so are some promises.

A mile and a half past the shelter, Moose and I come to our first river crossing. I can see the trail on the far side of the riverbank. There are a few stones braced against the current, but it will be impossible to cross without getting wet.

It's not a problem for Moose, though. He plunges into the river and is on the other side within a minute, shaking himself dry.

I kneel down and unlace my boots. I pull them off and peel my socks free from my feet. I stuff the socks deep into the boots, then tie the laces together and sling them around my neck. I roll up my pants as high as they will go, past my knobby knees and halfway up my thighs.

The stepping-stones are freezing cold. I curl my toes instinctively and brace myself against my trekking poles. Icy river water runs across my feet, then up my calves. I pick my way across the slippery crossing, wobbling a few times but never falling.

When I reach the other side of the river, I sit down and use my T-shirt to dry off my feet. My right hand shakes as it lifts a sock out of my boot, and I realize that I am trembling.

I finish putting on my boots and stand back up. I take slow, careful steps. From time to time, I lean on my trekking poles to take a break. When I feel like sitting down, Moose is always there to give me a nudge with his wet nose.

Even without thinking about my hunger, it is slow going. The trail is muddy and swollen with rain. I pick my way alongside giant boot-wrecker puddles. My feet squish into the muck and slurp from the suction as I pull them out.

My stomach had been growling, but now it is silent. It actually worries me. There's nothing left for it to grumble over. For the first time, I realize that even if I plan carefully, I could actually starve to death. I wonder if, after a while, the hunger pangs go away. If I'll ever stop being able to think about food. Because all I can think about now is that half a Snickers bar waiting in my side pocket. It taunts me, those beautiful peanut pieces embedded in delicious chocolate and sugary caramel. My mouth waters and every ten minutes, my fingers lurch toward it.

Wait, my mind tells me. *Wait until you really need it.*

The trail climbs up a gentle slope, then descends into a forest of weathered spruce and pine. I come to another river crossing. This one is a little deeper and a little colder, but I navigate it with less fear than my first.

When the trail begins a steep climb back up, I suppress a small groan and keep going. My pack straps begin to pull down on my shoulders.

Up, up, up. A brief view at the top of a small, rugged peak, then down again.

When the trail goes up again, I take a tiny nibble of Snickers bar. I am down to a third.

At the top of the next mountain, there is a small outcrop of rocks and a view of the valley below. I settle myself into sitting and take a look. What I see nearly makes me cry. At the bottom of the next valley is a real road. It glides west to east, like a smooth silvery lifeline.

CHAPTER 35

WHEN I TRY to stand up, my knees buckle underneath me. I lie there panting for a moment, my elbows bent as I prop myself up against the rocks.

It is time. I break out the last of my Snickers and let the chocolate and caramel and nougat dissolve slowly in my mouth. Only when the nubbins of the peanuts are bare do I chew. I give Moose two peanut pieces. He swallows them whole.

About two miles later, we come across a lean-to with shiny metal roofing and old weathered logs. I pause for a nap. Route 17 is less than five miles away.

We can make it.

We get four miles before coming upon the third river crossing. It's a turbulent one, with foaming white water churning above a swift current. There are no stepping-stones—it is all one high wall of angry water, high and fast, seething with mud and tree branches from two days' worth of storm.

Boots off. Socks off. Laces around my neck. Pants above

my knees. I know the drill by now. By the time I am standing at the river's edge, Moose is waiting for me on the other side.

The water nearly takes out my leg when I step into it. It is much, much stronger than the past two crossings. I grit my teeth and brace myself, moving in a long shuffle. The water rises to my shins, then my knees.

A sudden dip, and I am waist-high in water. The bottom of my pack is soaked.

There is a loud crack.

I look upstream and see a huge downed oak tree thrashing in the water. It is heading straight toward me, its branches dragging trails of grass and muck behind it.

I can't move fast enough. I see the thick, dark roots of the tree spread out like a net. It is going to nail me no matter what. *You're going to die*, I think.

Then I see Moose on the river's edge, barking his head off. "No, you're *not*," I tell myself.

It takes a lightning second to unloop my trekking poles from around my wrists and toss them. I unclip my pack and shrug it off into the river. It has kept me alive, but if I get caught with it under a tree in floodwaters, there is a very good chance that I will drown. Freed of my poles and my pack, I gulp a mouthful of air and plunge under the river just as the tree sweeps down upon me.

Churning water floods up my nostrils. My waterlogged boots hang at my neck like a noose. I half swim, half tumble as I feel the tree roots rake across my side. I twist by them and feel the trunk slide by, missing my head by inches.

Branches catch me on the arms and legs and scrape my ribs. They hit me in the stomach, nearly knocking out my mouthful of air. I kick hard against the bottom of the river, my bare feet scrabbling against the slime-covered stones.

I claw my way to the surface and take one big, sweet gulp of air. The bulk of the tree has passed me. I've made it.

I'm too shaken to swim properly, but I flounder my way to shallower water. I plant my feet on the ground. Here, toward the edge, the current is less brutal.

Then a stray branch at the top of the tree hooks itself around my laces and lifts my boots off my shoulders.

I grab the leather below the eyelets. "No!" I scream. I lean back and brace myself.

I am in a tug-of-war against an oak tree. I will not lose.

The laces tighten and it feels like my arms are being pulled from their sockets. There is a snap as the branch breaks. Drops of water fly free as I pull my boots to my chest, and the tree continues its journey downriver.

Clutching my boots, I wade to the far shore. Moose licks my face joyfully, and I shake off the river—the mud, the water, the rotting leaves and soaked moss. I remove my shirt and wring it out, then do the same for my pants. My socks are swollen and wet, but still lodged inside my boots. I take them out and squeeze out the water, then lay everything on a sloped boulder warmed by the early July heat.

As I wait for my clothes to dry, I walk down the river to look for my trekking poles and pack. I don't have much hope, but as I scan the water, I see a flash of blue nylon on the near bank.

By some miracle, my pack has floated into an eddy. I climb down the riverbank and pull it out. It is heavy and slumps wetly against the ground.

I drag it to the boulder where my clothes are and unclip the hood. Everything is completely waterlogged but still there.

I'm not going to make it to the road in this state. I am too weakened by hunger and the river to carry soaked gear another mile.

But I realize that somewhere outside my fog of hunger, it is a nice day. Lots of sun. Wearily, I lay all my gear out to dry. My sleeping bag, Lucas's tent, my extra clothes. My headlamp doesn't work, so I pry open the battery door and take out the batteries, hoping that some time in the sun will get the electrical bits working again.

The afternoon sun hits me hard. I curl up on the rock next to my stuff and drape a bit of tent flap over my face. I let the warmth of the July sun soak into my bones. I am tired. I am hungry. But I am not afraid.

The next thing I know, it is late evening. My boots are still a little damp, but the rest of my belongings are so sun-dried they crinkle like potato chips. I gather everything and put it all back in my pack, except for my sleeping pad and my bag, which I lay out on a soft piece of grass by the river. I've survived one night without shelter. I can survive another.

As I get into my sleeping bag, Moose walks over. He lays his head next to mine, and together we fall asleep under the stars.

The next morning, I wake to find my skin burning. My entire body has turned a deep sunburned pink. I press a spot on my arm. It fades white, but goes right on back to being lobster colored.

It hurts to put my backpack on. It feels like red-hot pokers are digging into my skin as the straps dig into my chest.

I will get to the road; I will get to a town, I chant over and over in my head as I walk. *I will get to the road; I will get to a town.*

Now it is less than a mile to the road. I am in pain, and my stomach is hurting so badly it feels like it is devouring itself.

I try to quiet my mind, to accept the pain of the trail, but not to despair or to give in to it. *I will get to the road; I will get to a town.*

I descend a final hill and break out of the trees, and there it is: Route 17.

My brain explodes in the victory dance that my body can't manage, but my celebration is brief.

I know it's only a few more miles into town, but I'm not sure I have the energy to take another step. As I am standing, unsteady on my feet and uncertain of what to do, a small red Toyota pickup truck comes rumbling down the road. It slows and pulls off a few yards in front of us. The passenger-side window rolls down, and a teenage girl with freckles across her tanned face leans out. "Hey there. You need a ride to town?"

I'm wary after my last hitchhiking attempt, but there's something about the girl's face that is kind. Trustworthy. I nod. "Can you take my dog, too?" My voice is scratchy and strange-sounding.

"Sure." The girl looks down at Moose. "Huh. That's funny."

"What is?" I am immediately on guard.

"I swear I've seen that dog before."

"Oh, I've had Moose since he was a puppy." The lie slips easily out of my mouth. When it comes to protecting Moose, I will do anything.

The girl shrugs. She thumbs over to the driver's seat, where an older man with a gray beard that travels all the way down to his belly button holds on to the steering wheel. "I'm Sadie and this here's my dad, Jim. We're going to the grocery store in Rangeley. We can take you as far as there."

"Are you heading back this way once you're done shopping?"

"Sure are. We can take you back here if you want." The girl's thumb travels to the open cab. "Hop on back."

I bring down the tailgate, and Moose jumps up into the cab. I sling up my pack and follow with my body a moment later. As I collapse against my bag, the truck rumbles to life, and we set off in the morning heat toward town.

▲

CHAPTER 36

AS WE PULL up to the parking lot of the grocery store, Moose whines uneasily. "Shh," I tell him. "I know you're hungry. Just wait. I'll have food for you soon enough."

After weeks on the trail, the glaring fluorescent lights and bright bleached floors of the grocery store catches me off guard, and I wince under the artificial lights and smells. But they don't stop me from rushing into the checkout lane and grabbing two Snickers bars from the candy display. I'm already tearing off the wrapper to one of them as the pony-tailed teenage cashier rings me up. I ignore her raised eyebrows as I simultaneously gobble down the bar and root in my pack for my money.

The first Snickers is gone before I've been handed my change. The second one disappears before my shopping cart has left the produce aisle. As I wander past shelves chock-full of food, I try not to let all the Little Debbies, the Ho Hos and Twinkies, the Nutty Bars and dozen packs of powdered doughnuts distract me. I've fed myself. Now it's time to think about feeding Moose.

I find the pet aisle and get yet another ten-pound bag of Purina for Moose. Then I turn around and begin to shop for my next couple of days on the trail. In addition to stocking up on dinner food, I pick up a three-pound bag of M&M'S, a family-sized pack of Nutty Bars, and a thirty-two-ounce tub of peanut butter. By the time I'm done, my shopping cart looks almost exactly like the basket I had at the Cumberland Farms gas station. I feel a sting of irritation at having to pay for groceries twice.

I eat the Nutty Bars as I unroll two twenties and pay at the checkout lane, muttering a small curse on the man in the sunglasses. Once again I ignore the ponytailed cashier, who by now is openly glaring at me, as though she's caught me picking my nose instead of eating food in a grocery store.

I tuck everything into the empty spaces of my pack and cinch the hood closed. As I put my remaining dollar bills back into the Ziploc, I pause for a second to count it. I have eighty-two bucks left. I gulp. That's only enough for two more resupplies, three if I really scrimp. I'm going to have to be careful about spending money from now on. Maybe I should have kept that sixty-seven cents at the last grocery store. It could have bought me most of a Snickers bar.

As I'm looking down at the last of my money, wild barking erupts from the parking lot. I know that sound. I drop everything and rush through the sliding glass doors into the hot summer air.

Someone is climbing into the cab of the red truck. He is tall and stocky, with a pockmarked face and a half-smoked cigarette dangling from his mouth. A wide, saggy beer gut hangs over his thick silver belt buckle. "Buster!" he shouts. "Shut up, Buster!"

Moose is backed up and crouching behind the wheel well. His claws scrabble against the plastic of the truck bed as he tries to mash himself into a tiny ball as far away from the man as he can get.

"Stop scaring him!" I have reached the truck. I put my hands on one side and a foot on a wheel to hoist myself up. I get halfway up when my arms give out on me. I tumble backward onto the parking lot. My hands hit the asphalt and I cry out as twin jolts of pain run up my wrists.

From the top of the truck bed the man looms up, at least a foot taller than me. He looks big. And mean. His sausage-sized fingers clench into a massive, hairy fist.

"Look here, boy," he says. His voice is ugly. "Buster here is mine. I don't know what you're doing with him, but you have no right to tell me how to talk to my own dog."

"He's not your dog!" The words escape my mouth before I can stop them. "I found him in the woods miles from here. I fed him and bathed him and took care of him. He's with me."

"Listen, you little toad. I've owned Buster for two years. Just because he decides he's going to run off don't make him yours."

"What's going on here, Lewis?" Jim has returned with a shopping cart full of groceries.

"Boy's trying to steal my dog, that's what!" shouts Lewis. "And what's he doing in the back of your truck?"

"Dad, what's going on?" Sadie has come out. She is holding a gallon of milk in one hand and a bag of potatoes in the other.

"Sadie, get back in the store," Jim says. "Lewis, what are *you* doing in my truck?"

Lewis draws himself up to his full height. "I am getting my dog back!" He reaches down and grabs Moose. Moose howls miserably.

"Lewis, calm yourself." Jim has let go of the shopping cart and has both of his hands up.

"Don't tell me to calm down, Jim. I'm taking Buster back to the farm. And you and this little hippie runt had better not try to stop me." Lewis jumps down from the cab, his arm crushing Moose's bruised side.

"Let him go!" I scream. Lewis is twice as big as me, but I don't care. I rush him. With a short, ugly laugh, he shoves me, and I hit the tar parking lot hard.

By the time I'm back on my feet Lewis is striding over to a rusting Ford pickup and tosses Moose inside. He climbs into the driver's seat and guns the engine. Tires squeal as he peels out of the parking lot and down the road.

"Hey. I'm sorry." Sadie has ignored her father and is right behind me. She puts her groceries down and pats my shoulder uncertainly.

My pack suddenly becomes a million pounds. I stagger against the tailgate and rest it against the bumper. I close my eyes and let fury and hatred mix all up in the pit of my stomach.

When I open them, I know what to do.

"I've got to get him back," I say.

Jim begins piling the groceries into the back of the truck. "That's not a good idea. Lewis has a bad streak. He won't take lightly to having Buster stolen."

"He ran away for a reason." I'm already trying to figure out a game plan. "When I found him, he was in horrible shape. He was starving. His hair was tangled and dirty. Part of it might have come from being on the trail, but he did not have a good owner to begin with."

"He's right, Dad." Sadie lifts the potatoes and the milk into the cab. "Everyone in town knows that Lewis treats Buster like dirt."

Jim shakes his head. "Still. It's not right to come between a man and his dog."

"I'm not asking for your help." And for once, I mean it. Moose is my responsibility. I brought him straight to the owner he'd tried to escape. And it's up to me to get him back. "All I need to know is where he lives. Just drop me off close to his home. That's all I want."

Jim folds his arms. "And what do you think you're going to be able to do once you get there?"

"I'll think of something."

Jim hesitates for a minute, then gives a long sigh. "Hop in."

I climb into the truck bed once more and rest my head against the back window as we pull out of the parking lot. My brain is buzzing with a bazillion ways to rescue Moose. I have visions of scoping out Lewis's home and returning in the middle of the night to free Moose from being chained to a doghouse or tree in the backyard. Calling to him through the window and having him break free of Lewis to be with me.

The truck slows to a crawl, then stops on a familiar piece of road.

"Hey. This is where you picked me up," I yell through the back window.

Jim rolls down the window and sticks out his head. "That's right. You get going now. There ain't nothing you can do for that dog."

I wait for a wave of helplessness to wash over me, like it has so many times before. The feeling of defeat and despair, of bad luck hammering down to remind me that I'm cursed and I can't do anything about it.

But those feelings don't come. Instead, for the first time, I feel something else. It fills me, thick and fast and powerful.

Rage.

"You don't know that!" I scream. I pound my fist on the back of the window. "I don't care if Lewis is twice my size, I've got to save Moose. Turn around. Take me back!"

"Son." Jim is calm. "I feel for you. But I'm not sending you to a crazy man's house so you can steal his dog."

"He's *my* dog!" I shriek. I slam my hands against the roof. "Take me back!"

Jim doesn't say anything. The truck idles as I bang the roof over and over and over again. I am so viciously angry I feel like I could punch a hole right into the truck.

Finally I toss my pack over the side and jump out of the cab. If Jim isn't going to drive me, I'll go and find Moose myself. I sling my pack on my shoulder and start marching back to town.

The truck pulls alongside me. "Kid," Jim says.

I don't look at him. I focus my eyes on the road.

"Kid, turn back. Or I'm gonna turn you into the police station. You gonna get yourself killed if you go after that dog, and I ain't gonna be responsible for that."

I stop. If I get turned in, I lose everything. Moose. The Trail. My promise to Lucas.

Everything.

My hands rise to my face and my fingernails bury themselves in my temples. I scream so loudly that a flock of birds rise from the trees and fly off in a panic.

I turn around. Away from town and from Moose and from any chance of saving him.

"Good luck with your hike, kid," Jim says.

Sadie doesn't look at me. She's busy scribbling away at a piece of notebook paper.

"Thanks for the ride," I say sarcastically.

As the Toyota drives away, a crumpled scrap of paper falls out of the passenger-side window.

I go over to pick it up. I tuck it into the Ziploc bag with my matches and the List and stuff it into the side of my pack. It'll be good starter for the next time I have a fire. Or feel like burning down the forest.

CHAPTER 37

I HAD PROMISED Moose I would take care of him. That he could depend on me. That he would be safe.

But instead I led him straight to a man who had starved and abused him. A man with big knuckles and a big belt buckle. Who threw Moose into his truck. Actually threw him.

I stop on the trail and lean against a tree, breathing in short gasps, trying so hard not to cry. I feel almost like I did when Lucas died. That heavy sick feeling is back, as though a gallon of slime has been poured down my throat. My stomach lurches.

I've failed another friend.

I'm not just bad luck; I put my friends in bad situations.

I don't remember how long I am there, grinding my forehead into the bark of the tree trunk, trying to erase the memory of Lewis throwing Moose into his truck. But no amount of physical pain is going to take back the past.

Finally I step away. I stare blankly in front of me. And then I begin to hike. Because I don't know what else to do.

The trail leaves the road and climbs through thick spruce forests. The steepness should slow me down, but instead I speed up until I'm nearly running. I have to get away from Moose and what I did to him. I race up a giant mountain, willing myself to go faster and faster.

The trail is muddy and full of roots and rocks. It's not fun at all to hike. I'm nearly at the top of a mountain when a guy comes toward me, his long arms and legs a blur of motion. He is tall and lanky and smells exactly like a thru-hiker—unwashed pits, dark-brown hair matted with sweat and grease, boots and calves stained with a thick layer of mud.

I huddle off to the side of the trail to let him through. Just like his pace, his eyes are manic. They stare straight ahead, calculating the dips and dives of the tricky footing of the trail in nanoseconds. He doesn't even see me. It's as if I'm no one.

It is dark by the time I reach a shelter. I set up and go to sleep, alone in my despair.

I deserve to be alone.

The next day I summit four peaks. The sky is blue and the views are clear, but I don't care. I've lost Moose, and no amount of fine weather is going to make me feel better. As evening falls I descend a long, rocky hill and break out of the trees onto a real road. There is a car parked on the side of the trail. A Subaru Outback with the hatch flipped up. Sitting in the back, their feet swinging, are a man and a woman. A beat-up red Coleman cooler rests between them.

The man has bright blue eyes and a grizzly beard. The woman is plump and deeply suntanned, with kind brown eyes.

As I get closer, I see a piece of paper duct taped to the cooler. On it are two words handwritten in permanent marker. Two simple words: "Trail Magic."

When the man sees me, he waves me over. When he opens the cooler, I peer in and see soda cans scattered in ice. I reach straight for a Coke. The dark fizzy liquid hits my tongue and I want to weep. The instant sugar is making my head light, so I drink slowly, burping with appreciation.

The woman hands me a sandwich. "Here you go, dear," she says. Turkey and mayo, tomato, and lettuce between two slices of homemade bread studded with sesame seeds and oats. I blink and chew.

The man watches me eat. "Marsha, get the fellow another one," he says when I am done.

The woman hands me another sandwich. It is gone in a few hurried mouthfuls.

After I finish the Coke, the man pulls out a gallon jug of water and hands it to me. "You're lookin' a little parched."

"Thank you, sir."

The man nods. "Name's Clyde," he says.

"Tony." I am grateful for Clyde and Marsha, but it doesn't stop me from being wary about my name again. "Thanks for all this."

"Least we can do. Our son, Alex, started thru-hiking two months ago. You must be his age, or a little younger. What are you, fifteen?"

I realize that after only a few weeks on the trail, I already seem a lot older than I am.

I nod, not wanting to tell Clyde my real age.

"Alex is seventeen. We made him a promise that we'd set up some Trail Magic every Sunday until he finished. Figured it'd be good luck for him." Clyde points to the water. "Have the whole thing—we've got five more gallons and'll be packin' up in about an hour. Don't think we're in any danger of runnin' out."

I slug back a quarter of it before refilling my empty water bottles.

"Oh, honey." Marsha touches my arm gently and I wince. She frowns. "You've got a wicked sunburn, too. I've got something for that." She reaches behind into the magical backseat and brings out a bottle of aloe vera gel.

I pump some of the gooey green liquid into my hand. As I spread it across my reddened skin, soothing coolness travels across me.

"Keep the bottle. And take as much food as you want," says Clyde.

"Hon, do you need a night off the trail?" Marsha asks me. I can feel her eyes on me. They are warm. Motherly.

▲

She points to a white clapboard house with green shutters and a screened porch just down the road. "We live right there. You could spend the night with us, if you'd like."

I am tired. I am sore. The next shelter is five miles away, and I have only another hour before dark. All I want to do is curl up in a real bed and cry.

But I also don't want to accept any help. After losing Moose, I don't deserve help. I'm just about to tell Clyde and Marsha no when my eyes fall on my pack. If I don't take some time off the trail to fix my gear, I'm going to be in trouble. I have to repair the tent in case I can't make it to shelters on the remote stretches of trail through the Maine woods. Seal up the gash in my sleeping pad. Get more iodine pills. Maybe some more food. I need to be smart.

I decide to compromise. "That's awful kind of you. I don't want to be too much of a bother, though. Could I just sleep on your porch tonight?"

"Of course." Marsha smiles. "You go on right ahead. Clyde and I will be there in an hour. Door's open if you want to use the bathroom or anything."

I thank them and head over to the house. As twilight falls, I set my pack on the porch, and I switch on the porch light and settle cross-legged on wooden decking with my belongings. There is a patch kit in a small pocket in the sack of my air pad. I take out a circular patch and a thin tube of glue. I cover the gash in my pad with the patch and set it aside to dry.

Next, I take a look at the tent poles. They really are badly mangled—I can't save them. I think about how they were pieces of the shelter that was going to keep Lucas and me safe and dry on the trail.

I can't give up Lucas's tent. I need to have something of his with me when I reach Katahdin. I take the broken tent poles and roll them up in the tent fabric. I open the tent bag and place everything inside. I'll find a way to make it shelter me, somehow.

As I'm cinching the tent bag closed, I notice the Ziploc with my matches and Sadie's tossed-away crumple of paper. I open the bag and check the matches. They are still dry. Good.

The paper is dry as well. I smooth it out to refold it into a neat square to tuck into my hood pocket. And that's when I see it.

Sadie hadn't thrown away a piece of scrap paper. She had drawn me a map to Moose.

CHAPTER 38

IT IS A detailed map, with the Rangeley grocery store as a central marker. Past the grocery store, Route 4 heads east for several miles before a side road branches off into a cluster of back roads.

It is at one of these back roads that Sadie has made a stick house with the word "BUSTER" hastily scribbled over it. There is also a phone number.

I stare at the rumpled paper and realize that I have been given a choice. I can continue on the trail and finish what Lucas and I started. I can tick off number ten on the List and keep my promise to my dead best friend.

Or I can go back to save a dog.

It's the hardest decision that I've had to make. I don't want to give up on either Lucas or Moose.

For a second, I wonder if Lucas's voice will come back into my head to tell me what to do. To lead me to the right choice. Instead, I hear nothing.

Then, in the stillness of the night, I see a flicker of light. And another. And another.

Fireflies. They appear in the field, magical little blinks that light up the field like it's Christmas.

I remember the last time I saw them. Lucas and I had set up camp in his backyard and had watched them come out as we talked about hiking the trail together. It had been just a few days before the quarry accident.

I had been so worried that something would go wrong, that we wouldn't finish, that it would all end in disaster. Finally Lucas had said, "You know what, Toe? It doesn't matter if we get to Katahdin. What matters is that it's going to be you and me, two friends having the adventure of a lifetime."

I gaze out at the fireflies. They are like little flashes of hope in the night.

That was it. I didn't have to finish the trail to prove to Lucas that he meant so much to me. Just being out here, being on this adventure was enough.

I had started the trail to get over the guilt that had weighed down my every step since last summer. But then I met Sean and Denver. They had taught me that, just like how Denver wasn't responsible for Harry's accident, I wasn't responsible for Lucas's death. Lucas made a choice, and so did I. I will always miss him, but he was the one who dove into the water.

Then I think about Wingin' It and his story. How his friend came back for him. Because that's what friends do.

I know what I have to do next.

I fold up the paper and tuck it in my pocket. There's a wooden shed housing a few metal trash cans next to the driveway. I pick up Lucas's broken tent and walk off the porch and to the shed. I open a can and carefully lay the tent inside.

As I walk back to the house, Clyde and Marsha pull into the driveway. I ask Marsha if I can use her phone. I dial ten numbers. After the fifth ring, a girl's voice answers. "Hello?"

"Hi, Sadie. This is Toby. I found your map. I'm coming to get Moose."

"Hold on a sec." There is silence on the other end, and then Sadie's voice comes back on. "When can you get here?"

"I think I'm about twenty-five miles away from Rangeley. I can get there tomorrow."

I hear some yelling in the background. Sadie's voice comes over, hushed and urgent. "Toby, I've got to go. If you can, give me a call when you're close tomorrow."

"I'll try." I hang up the phone and return it to Marsha. By the end of the evening, all my things are packed away, I've taken a good hot shower, and I have a promise from Clyde to drive me to Rangeley the next morning. I crawl into my sleeping bag and fall asleep to the sounds of crickets.

That night I dream that Moose has become a snarling wolverine, and Lewis a twelve-foot troll. They hunt me through a dark forest with trees oozing sticky black blood, down a trail scattered with broken tent poles as white as bone. They corner me against the rotting roots of a dead tree. Lewis aims a pitchfork at my heart. "My dog," he screams. I wake covered in sweat. It takes me a long time to settle back down to sleep.

The next morning I wake to the smell of bacon and eggs. Clyde opens the door and looks down at me. "You're coming in to have breakfast," he tells me. It is an order. I go in.

"How did you sleep, honey?" Marsha is in the kitchen in front of the stove. She fills a plate of crispy warm bacon and scrambled eggs glistening with butter and gives it me with a fork.

"Okay." I don't tell her about the nightmare as I sit down at the table.

Marsha fills a tall glass with orange juice and sets it in front of me. "Well, once you finish up here, Clyde can take you into town. He's aiming to leave around nine."

An hour later Clyde and I are rumbling into Rangeley. It is a fine, warm day. Clyde rolls down the windows and I stick my hand out, letting the wind stream through my fingers.

When we get into town, I ask to borrow Clyde's phone, and with it I dial Sadie's number.

"Where are you?" Sadie asks when she hears my voice.

"The grocery store in Rangeley," I tell her.

"I'll meet you at Keep's Corner Café. It's about a mile west of you on Route Sixteen."

Five minutes later we pull into the café. I hop out of the truck and go over to the driver's side. Clyde shakes my hand. "Good luck, Tony," he says to me.

I lean over and give him a hug through the window. "Thanks for everything, Clyde."

"You take care, young man," he tells me. He puts the truck in gear and rumbles away.

I am alone again. But not for long. I am going to get Moose back. It's the only promise that matters now.

CHAPTER 39

AN HOUR LATER, Sadie comes into the café. She gets a coffee and I get hot chocolate. We order two cinnamon rolls and pull up two chairs around a table to talk.

I have to ask the question. It has been bugging me ever since finding that map of Lewis's place. "Why are you helping me?"

Sadie bites into a roll. "This is the north country. Up here you're taught to leave your neighbors alone. Not to butt in, even if you see something that's wrong. We respect one another's privacy and right to do whatever we want. But Lewis has been abusing that dog ever since he got him.

"I remember the first time I was riding my bike past his place when he came raging out of his house holding Buster by the scruff of his neck." Sadie's eyes darken. "He threw Buster. He threw him off the front porch, and Buster hit the dirt.

"I've never forgotten the way he yelped, and the way he whined when Lewis came off the porch to get him. I stopped and yelled at Lewis. I told him that was no way to treat a dog. Lewis told me oh yes it was if the dog pissed on your floor. I told him that's what puppies do, they don't know any better, and Lewis said he was gonna make sure that Buster would know better next time. And he told me to mind my business or I was gonna get it."

Sadie takes a swig of coffee. "You've seen Lewis. He's a big guy. I was afraid. I pedaled away and left him with Buster lying in the dirt. That was two years ago. Since then I haven't seen Lewis say one kind word to that dog, or give him more than curses and kicks. If there's someone who's willing to take Buster away, I'm gonna help 'em. And that someone looks to be you."

I nod. "What do you know about Lewis?" I ask. "Do you think he's home right now?"

Sadie asks me for the map she drew. When I show it to her, she points to the stick drawing of the house. "Lewis grows corn across the road from his house. Usually he's out on his tractor during the day.

"If we can get there soon, the farmhouse should be empty. We can find Buster and get him out of there before Lewis returns home." Sadie nods toward the door. "I've got my four-wheeler outside. You ready?"

I pick up my pack and heft it onto my shoulders. "Ready."

We put our dirty plates in a brown plastic tub and head out. Sadie's four-wheeler is parked across the street.

Sadie has brought a few bungee cords and she swings them in the air. "Take your bag off and relax for a second." I hand her my pack and she lashes it to the black metal bars on the back of the four-wheeler. As I roll my neck, she asks, "What are you going to do when you get Buster back?"

I have been thinking about this a lot. "Part of me wants to finish the Appalachian Trail. I . . . had a promise I wanted to keep to a friend." I shake my head. "But I'm going to go home. Moose needs some love and attention. Real dog food. Rest. I will hike the trail. But I'm going to do it when he's ready. And when he is, I'll be, too."

Sadie swings a leg around the front the vehicle. "Hop on," she tells me.

I climb behind her and grip the bars under the pack. Sadie turns her head. "No. You gotta grab onto my waist. And hold tight. We've got bumps ahead."

I wrap my arms around Sadie as she flips a switch on the four-wheeler. The engine rumbles to life, and we are off with a jolt.

After a few miles, Sadie turns off the main drag onto a narrow dirt road. The motor thunks when she switches it off. "Lewis's place is a half mile farther," she says.

I hop off the four-wheeler and decide to leave my pack behind so I can be light on my feet for the rescue. We make our way down the road to an old, ramshackle farmhouse with faded white paint. Ivy chokes the rain gutters and creeps down the corners of the house.

I look across the road, to a large field covered in corn, their silk tassels rustling in the summer wind. I spot a big straw hat in the middle of the rows.

Lewis.

I nudge Sadie and point to the hat. She nods and we duck around to the back of the farmhouse, out of sight of the cornfields. There is a half-falling-down barn with moldy, rotting shingles and a sagging roof out back.

And then I see him. Attached by a thick iron chain to a pole in the ground. Panting in the sun, with no shade. Or water. Collapsed on the ground and barely breathing. Moose.

I forget to hide. I break out from the side of the house and run to him. He struggles to his feet when he sees me, but something is wrong with one of his legs. He is limping, his right paw up.

My vision goes red with rage. I unclip his collar from the chain. "C'mon, Moose. I'm getting you out of here."

"Are you now?" I turn around. Lewis is in the farmhouse, grinning at me through an open window.

For a second, I refuse to believe it's him. I've seen his straw hat. Saw it bobbing in the fields across the street.

And then it comes to me. Scarecrows in cornfields also have straw hats.

Lewis reaches down with one hand. When he brings it up, it is holding a shotgun. He rests the long barrel against the windowpane and trains the muzzle straight at me. "You are trespassing, you no-good, dog-stealing runt. I have every right to blow you away."

"Lewis, don't!" cries Sadie. She runs out and stands between me and the gun. "We'll leave, promise. We won't give you no trouble."

"Hey, Lewis." My heart is thumping like a jackrabbit's, so hard I'm afraid it'll burst out of my chest. But my hands are steady. "Hey, Lewis. I've got a deal for you."

I reach into my pocket and take out my Ziploc with my trail money. I had hoped to make a clean getaway with Moose, but it was time for plan B. I hold up the money and wave it in the air. "What do you say I buy Moose from you? I've got eighty-two dollars. If I give you every last penny I have, will you give him to me?"

Lewis lowers his gun for a moment. Then he shakes his head and retrains it on Sadie and me. "First of all, this here dog's name is Buster. Not Moose. Second of all, your money's mighty tempting, but you're not getting my dog. He's *mine*." The last word is accompanied by the click of the shotgun hammer as Lewis removes the safety.

Plan C, plan, C, plan C!!! my brain screams. I don't have a plan C, but words start tumbling out of my mouth. "Well, how about this. We have a contest. We put Moo— Buster between the two of us and call to him. If he comes to me, I get him. But if he goes to you, you get him—and all my money, too."

Lewis works over the details in his head. It takes him a while. "So if Buster comes to me, I get my dog *and* your money?" He lowers the shotgun and smiles. "You got yourself a deal, kiddo."

CHAPTER 40

WE FACE OFF behind the farmhouse. Sadie draws a line in the dirt with her toe and tells me to stand behind it. She counts ten paces, scuffs out a center mark, counts ten more paces. She draws another line in the dirt with her toe, and Lewis swaggers over to it.

Sadie gently takes Moose by the collar and leads him to the scuffed-out center mark. "When I count to three, I'm going to let go. Both of you do what you think you gotta to do to get this dog behind your line. No moving one toe over your line. B——

"One, two, three!"

I can do this. I crouch down and lay my elbows against my knees. "Here, Moose! Here, boy!"

On the other end, Lewis's voice booms out. "Buster! Get yer mangy butt over here!"

Moose looks back and forth between us. His tail thumps the ground uncertainly.

"BUSTER!" Lewis stomps his foot on the ground.

Moose plasters his ears against his head and whines.

Lewis jerks his finger down and points toward the dirt beside him. "NOW!" His fixes Moose with a stare so vile, so full of anger and hate, that Moose's legs buckle, leaving him cowering on the ground.

I thought this would be easy, but now I'm starting to realize how powerful fear is. What if Moose is so scared of Lewis that he won't disobey him? I hadn't truly thought that Moose might go anywhere but straight to me.

I'm not giving up, though. "Hey, Moose. Hey." My voice is nowhere near as powerful as Lewis's. Or as commanding. I clap my hands, trying to distract Moose from Lewis's hypnotizing glare.

One of Moose's ears perks up. It's as if he can hear me, but from an ocean away.

"You scruffy flea-ridden mutt!" screams Lewis. "If you don't get yourself over here right now, you're gonna wish you were never born."

Moose whines. He hears the venom in Lewis's voice. And the promise of violence. He starts to slink toward Lewis.

"That's what I thought, you ugly cur. C'mon." Lewis reaches his hands out.

"Moose, no!" I am about to lose everything. All my promises. All my hope. I start to take a step forward.

"Get back behind the line, you filthy maggot!" Lewis's fingernails are inches from Moose's collar. He glares at me.

He's no longer looking at Moose.

My foot hovers, an inch from the line.

"Back!" Lewis bellows.

I step back and whistle. Moose, free of Lewis's gaze, perks up his ears and swings his head toward me. I can see the whites of his eyes. "Moose," I say. "Moose. Buddy. Listen to me. You don't belong here. This isn't your home. I am your home." My voice cracks. "Hey, Moose. Hey. I love you."

Moose turns. He straightens up and starts to move back toward me and my heart soars—and then Lewis makes a grab for him. Moose swerves and dodges, avoiding Lewis's big hands, and in a few hobbled bounds he is over to me and I've got my arms around his neck and my face buried in his fur.

"Good Moose," I say. "Good dog."

"He chose Toby!" Sadie shouts. "Deal's a deal."

Lewis doesn't answer. He turns toward the farmhouse, and even though I want to believe that he's going to be true to his word and will let me and Moose and Sadie go, I know that he's going for his shotgun.

I pick up Moose. "Run," I tell Sadie.

We flee past the house and down the dirt road. Moose is heavy in my arms, but it doesn't stop me from running faster than I ever have in my life. I hear cursing behind me, foul words that singe my ears like flamethrowers. I look back. Lewis is on his front porch, the shotgun stock braced against his hip. He pumps it once.

I tackle Sadie, and we both go down. I arch sideways, keeping Moose from hitting the ground as my shoulder absorbs the impact.

Lewis fires the gun. There's a roar, and dirt kicks up twenty feet away from us. "Give me back my dog!" he screams. He throws his gun down and starts toward us.

Sadie pulls me up. "C'mon."

Adrenaline explodes through my veins. My shoulder aches, but I barely feel it. I focus on the road. My breath is even. My legs move like pistons. The endurance and strength I have built over the weeks on the trail steady me as I sprint forward, a twenty-pound dog clutched in my arms.

We make it to the four-wheeler. Lewis is thirty yards behind us, but closing fast. Sadie yanks on the starter rope. The engine sputters and dies.

Sadie yanks again. The motor catches and rumbles to life. She hurtles onto the seat. "Get on!" she yells. Lewis has ten yards before he is on us.

I swing behind Sadie, one hand around her waist, the other wrapped around Moose. Sadie throws the four-wheeler into first and slams on the gas just as Lewis reaches us. I glance behind me and see a meaty hand slam onto my tied-down backpack.

"Faster!" I yell as Sadie switches into second. I look back. Hand over hand, Lewis is climbing over my backpack and onto the four-wheeler.

There is no time to think. I let go of Sadie and twist around, unhooking the bungee cords keeping my pack in place. The cords whip through the rack, and suddenly they are free and tumbling off the four-wheeler, along with my pack and Lewis.

Sadie hits third, and my heart begins to slow as Moose's former owner fades into the distance.

I let out a wild scream of victory.

I've got my dog back.

As I ride along the bumpy road, I glance down at this dog. I think about Lucas. And the trail. And promises—the ones that were meant to be kept. And the ones that turned into other promises.

It's not about finishing the trail. It's about finding what's important in life and fighting for it. It's about friendship and adventure and realizing how strong you can be.

Back at Sadie's house, I ask to use her phone. I dial a number I know by heart.

"Hello?"

"Hi, Gran." My voice nearly breaks. "I'm ready to come home."

After I hang up the phone, there's one more thing I have to do. I fumble in my pocket and pull it out. It's weather-beaten and beyond crumpled, but the words are still so clear. Almost all of them are crossed out.

There's a cup full of pens on the kitchen counter. I take one and go outside with Moose. Together we walk until the woods surround us, where all I can see are trees with their summer green leaves and the unmarked ground ahead of me. Unlike the Appalachian Trail, there is no path to follow, no white blazes to show me the way.

I take the List and rest it against the bark of an old oak tree. The tip of the pen touches *#10*, and I draw one long, unbroken line.

It's time to make my own trail.

ACKNOWLEDGMENTS

A huge thank-you to my editor, Emily Seife, who brought this book to life with her keen eye and unflinching red pen. Toby's story is so much richer because of you.

Thanks to Beth Weick and Anna Sysko for providing Appalachian Trail maps for me to pore over and mark Toby's journey, day by day.

When I needed to do firsthand research, Emile Hallez was my stalwart hiking and backpacking partner. Thank you for carrying the heavy tent (and that pesky one-pound jar of peanut butter) through our mountain adventures.

Finally, a quiet, bone-deep thank-you to my father, Toshio Hashimoto. You gave me the gift of the mountains, a gift for which I will be ever grateful.